SHEILA SPENCER-SMITH

THE LEMON TREE

Complete and Unabridged

LINFORD
Leicester

First published in Great Britain in 2017

First Linford Edition
published 2018

*A catalogue record for this book is available
from the British Library.*

ISBN 978–1–4448–3619–6

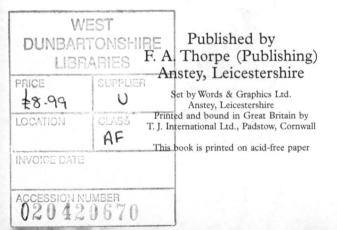
Published by
F. A. Thorpe (Publishing)
Anstey, Leicestershire

Set by Words & Graphics Ltd.
Anstey, Leicestershire
Printed and bound in Great Britain by
T. J. International Ltd., Padstow, Cornwall

This book is printed on acid-free paper

THE LEMON TREE

When her boyfriend Charles suggests they spend two months apart, Zoe's brother Simon invites her to come stay with him and his wife Thea in the idyllic village of Elounda on Crete, where they run a taverna. There Zoe meets Adam, an English tour guide. But business at the taverna isn't exactly brisk, and Adam will be leaving soon. Can Zoe make things work, or will she decide to return to her old life and Charles?

1

Zoe looked down at the letter in her hand, folded the paper with care and replaced it in the envelope. Across the room, Charles watched her. She looked up and saw him. This was a bad dream, and in a moment she would wake up and Charles would smile that long sweet smile of his.

But it didn't happen. Instead he got up and came towards her as if it pained him to do so. 'Zoe?' he said.

Something was wrong, and yet a flicker of relief surprised her. Shock, perhaps, that it had come to this when she hadn't been expecting it but had come to his sister's buffet lunch party prepared to feel as if she were almost one of the family. It had certainly seemed as if she were, by the way Charles had talked to her of his parents, implying that they were travelling down from the north in the expectation of meeting her.

'Charles?'

'You've read it?' His voice was unusually low.

'Not here, Charles. Not here in this crowded room.'

He caught her elbow and steered her towards the patio door that stood open to the evening breeze. The family party was ending now, people saying their farewells, kissing each other, hugging.

'Over here,' Charles said.

The sweet climbing rose on the arch was so rampant that it afforded the privacy they needed. He turned to her, his face solemn. 'I didn't know the best way to do this,' he said.

'But why, Charles, why? I thought . . . ' It was hard to voice her bewilderment without dissolving into humiliating tears. She hadn't seen it coming, that was all. 'I don't think there is a good way.'

'No.' His voice was strained.

Quite suddenly she felt sorry for him. Breaking up was never easy even for the trial period of two months that he wanted.

'Charles, please,' she said, 'don't look like that. I . . . I'll try to understand.'

'You will?'

For a moment he said nothing more, and she had time to think how it would be without Charles in her life even for a short period. But she couldn't, she couldn't . . .

'I think we need this time apart,' he added, almost pleadingly. 'We have to be sure it's right for both of us. It's sensible, don't you see?'

Sensible? she thought. It seemed like rejection to her.

'I could go right away,' he said. 'I could try and get some time off, I suppose, but we're a bit busy at the moment.'

'Where would you go?'

He shrugged. 'I'm not sure. But you, Zoe, have relations abroad, don't you? Your brother, I forget his name.'

'I need to think.'

'Of course. Me too. But it doesn't matter.'

She hesitated, and then with a great effort she smiled. It mattered to her a great deal to know where Charles was, but she wasn't going to say so. She turned away from him and pulled a branch of the climbing rose towards her and plucked a perfect bloom to hold close to her like a shield.

'Zoe?'

She blinked away more threatening tears before turning to face him. Until a few moments ago she had been happy, but that happiness had been built on nothing and she hadn't known it. Now she had to come to terms with something she wouldn't have believed could happen.

'I was thinking that some time apart would be useful, Zoe,' he said, his voice gentle. 'To give us the chance to get things in perspective.'

She nodded. What choice had she when it came down to it? Charles had made up his mind, and refusing to go along with it would make things even worse. She had sense enough to see that, even if she felt caught up in some nightmarish dream.

'And you agree?'

When she nodded, his relief was obvious in his posture, his voice. In everything. It was mortifying to see it. She straightened too, and smiled as she handed him the rose. The effort was nearly her undoing. She swallowed hard and held her head up high. 'I agree.'

'Thank you, Zoe.'

Again she turned from him, but this time she was walking across the lawn and out of the garden gate that led into the narrow road at the side of the house.

★ ★ ★

Zoe Harrison, twenty-four and a supply teacher much in demand in primary schools in the city of Bristol, wasn't going to fall apart because her boyfriend of eight months suggested a time away from each other for a while. At least that was her intention. But now, looking down at her shaking hands and only too aware of a tightening in her throat, she began to wonder.

She was heading for the floating harbour, always a solace in times of trouble. On the bridge she stopped so suddenly that she was in danger of causing a nasty incident only avoided by the quick side-stepping of the person behind her.

'Oh, sorry,' she muttered.

This wouldn't do. Two months, Charles said. It would pass.

She gazed across the water to the buildings on the other side, at the restaurant on ground level with its crowds of customers overflowing to the tables in the open air. The sky was overcast and a chill wind stirred her fly-away hair. There were boats moored, flags flying, and the sound of some raucous music that hurt her ears as much as the traffic noise behind her. Once she would have loved all this. Not now.

Maybe it would be best to go away from familiar scenes for a while. There was nothing to hold her here. The maternity leave she was filling in for was at an end, and she hadn't yet been asked to go somewhere else. She had no money worries, as she had been saving regularly for a rainy day, and that rainy day could be here. Her top-floor flat in her parents' Brislington home would still be there on her return.

The sun emerged from behind a cloud and the water in the basin seemed to sparkle suddenly. *A good omen*, she thought. *Well done, Zoe!*

She smiled as she left the bridge and waited for a gap in the traffic so she could cross the road in safety. She was being positive and that was good. She must accept that this could be the end between Charles and herself, whatever he said about a trial two months. What did that mean, exactly? That he had grown tired of her and wanted to check that this was really so before making the final decision? The End. That sounded final, and she wouldn't think of it.

She thrust her shoulders back and

held her head high as she took a final check to left and right and crossed the road.

★ ★ ★

That night Zoe couldn't sleep. Over and over in her mind went the traumatic scene in the garden when she had read that fateful letter and learned that Charles wanted them to have a break from each other.

She wondered now how he had explained her sudden departure from the party, her rushing off without expressing thanks for a lovely evening. It was impolite to say the least. This was the first time she had met his family en masse, and as such was an important event. So how would Charles explain her swift exit . . . sudden illness on her part? He didn't believe in lying, but he might have done so in this case to save face on behalf of them both. And for his sister's sake too, come to think of it. She wouldn't want to think that anyone was unhappy at her party, least of all her brother.

Zoe's heart felt sore now as she tried to think back over the last few weeks for any hint that things might have changed between Charles and herself. There had been nothing, she was sure of it. All right, she thought, there was that time in Bath when they were walking towards the Pump Room and his thoughts had seemed a long way off. She had thought nothing of it at the time, but now she wondered. But it was after that when Charles phoned to say he had invitations for them both to his colleague's engagement party. His voice had quickened with excitement as he described the narrowboat that was the venue for this important event.

'You will come? I thought you'd be surprised, Zoe. And pleased too, I hope.'

She was, and told him so.

'Old clothes, that's the dress code.'

'How old?'

'Anything that doesn't matter too

much. Can you manage that?'

'Of course.' She had been intrigued, as he had known she would, and he had fed her interest by describing days out he had had when he and Rob were boys together and Rob's parents had owned their own boat on the Kennet and Avon canal. It seemed he wanted her to know every detail and she had listened with amusement, loving his enthusiasm and obvious wish for her to be there too. The party had been a happy event, and afterwards Charles had been particularly loving. It was a day to remember with pleasure for years to come. Or so she had imagined.

Had he had his suspicions then that they weren't right for each other and was putting on an act? Or was he trying to convince himself that his feelings hadn't changed when at the back of his mind lurked the suspicion that he felt differently about her now? True, he had seemed relaxed and happy. She had liked to think she was attuned to people's feelings, but what did she know? Very little, it seemed.

The pain seemed to shoot up her body and then down again. What sort of teacher was she if she couldn't even do that? She had thought she understood Charles, who was close to her. She had been wrong, and that mattered a great deal.

2

To emerge from the bustle of Heraklion Airport on Crete into the warm dawn of an early summer day and see a notice with her name written on it beneath the word 'Welcome' was a huge surprise.

'That's me,' she said, going forward and dragging her suitcase-on-wheels behind her. 'I'm Zoe Harrison.'

The dark-haired man holding the board smiled. '*Kalimera*, Zoe. Good morning. I have come to meet you.' He pulled a note from the pocket of his shorts and handed it to her.

'*This is Thea's brother, Dimitri*,' she read in her brother's strong handwriting. '*He's a good driver and you can trust him to get you to us safely. We're caught up in something and have sent him instead. See you soon. Love from Thea and me, Simon.*'

She looked up. 'Dimitri?'

He bowed slightly, and when he straightened she saw that his brown eyes were laughing at her. She laughed too. 'I'm afraid I don't speak any Greek,' she said, 'yet. But I want to learn. *Kalimera*, I shall remember that.'

'*Efharisto*,' he said. 'Thank you. That is good.' His delighted smile illuminated his face. 'I think you will learn quickly.'

With Dimitri teaching her, she might find it easier than she imagined, she thought as she relinquished her case and her hand luggage to him and got into his car. He exuded confidence and concern that was reassuring. His open-necked blue shirt set off his smooth tan, and his smile was so infectious she found herself smiling too as they drove out of the airport and joined the traffic heading east on the wide highway. The sea was a silk sheet of palest blue, and the rim of the orange sun appeared above the horizon.

'It's beautiful,' she breathed.

'You have travelled a long way to see

a Crete dawn. You like it?'

'Yes, oh yes.'

The mountains on their right were emerging clearly now from their hazy mauve. The day was all before her in this new place she had wanted so much to see as soon as she knew that her brother and his new wife, Thea, were contemplating taking over the family taverna on Crete. As the light strengthened into full glorious daylight, she settled back to enjoy the journey in the company of someone who kept up a flow of amusing information about the rugged mountains and glimpse of distant villages they passed. Although the windows were closed for the air conditioning to function, Zoe could imagine the scent of the wild thyme floating in to them. Pink and white oleander bushes lined the road and the central reservation. When at last they reached the town of Agios Nikolaos overlooking the azure sea, Zoe drew in a breath of pure pleasure.

'You like it?' Dimitri said. 'It takes a

little longer, but we've driven through it for you to see.'

'Thank you,' she said. '*Efharisto*, Dimitri. You are kind.'

He threw her an appreciative smile. 'One day I show you more.'

They passed white hotels and apartments outlined against the vivid sky and took the road out of the town and up and over more rugged high ground. *I haven't given Charles a thought for two whole hours*, she thought, marvelling.

At last they drove down a steep hill and through a smaller town. Zoe glimpsed narrow streets, a riot of colourful boats in the harbour, palm-fringed sand and glittering sea. Backing it all, the mountains looked enticingly close. Excitement bubbled up inside her. She was here at last, and soon she would see her brother Simon and Thea, his bride of ten months.

'We are nearly there now,' Dimitri said, turning his head a little to smile at her.

Even at this early hour, daily life was beginning to stir. Shutters were rattling up; someone was arranging wooden chairs round a table on the pavement helped by a young child staggering under a weight of cushions.

'It all looks so colourful and fresh,' she said. 'I wish we could stop and look at it all properly.'

He laughed. 'Your wish will be granted another day.'

She laughed too. His friendliness charmed her.

The Lemoni Taverna was almost at the water's edge. Only a road divided it from the pavement on the other side and a short drop down to a narrow strip of beach and the inviting stretch of calm sea beyond.

Dimitri blasted his horn as he drew up by a low wall. A moment's pause to calm the fluttering of her heart, and then Zoe opened her door and stepped out into air that enveloped her like a warm duvet. At once she felt disorientated, unable to believe that she was really here in this place she had heard so much about ever since Simon had become engaged to a girl from Crete.

She saw the shady courtyard and smelt the faint dusty scent of vegetation and immediately felt welcome.

And here Simon was as big and smiling as ever. 'Great to see you, Zoe,' he said in his booming voice. 'Welcome to the Lemoni.' He ducked beneath an overhanging olive branch and enveloped her in a huge hug. He smelt warm and familiar, although they hadn't seen each other for several months. But Simon was like that — best friends with everybody, especially his own family.

She was aware of Dimitri carrying her suitcase and placing it nearby, and then of the sound of his car driving off. 'I haven't thanked him,' she murmured as Simon released her.

Simon gave a deep, throaty laugh. 'He'll be back sometime. So will Thea. I'm ordered to show you your room and let you rest. But first some refreshment?'

Her answer was a yawn and a quick apology.

He laughed again. 'We'll take a bottle of water from the fridge up with us.

Come this way, Zoe. We'll have a huge talk later, not now. Bed for you, and a long sleep.'

He lifted her suitcase as if it was full of air. She was hardly aware of the dim passageway, the staircase, the opening of a door at the end and the cool dark room. She saw only the low bed and felt the tiled floor beneath her feet.

Simon placed her luggage by the wall. The bottle he placed on a small cabinet. He looked round for a drinking vessel and, not seeing one, shrugged.

'That's fine,' she said, yawning again and rubbing her eyes. 'I don't need a glass, Simon.'

He nodded. 'Keep the shutters closed,' he said and was gone.

Zoe lay down on the bed and fell instantly asleep.

★ ★ ★

The sounds outside when she woke told Zoe at once where she was, and for a few blissful moments she lay listening to the Greek voices, the evocative music from somewhere nearby, the laughter outside and in the background muted traffic noises. So different from home and so stimulating.

She looked at her watch in the dim light. Twenty-five minutes past two in the afternoon, Greek time. That meant just past midday at home. Not as bad as she had feared but bad enough.

She got up slowly and then enjoyed a long, cool shower. The bathroom was the room next to hers, thankfully. Back in her room, wrapped in a voluminous towel, she looked round for her case to dig out some fresh light clothes. The rest of her unpacking could wait. Time enough to unpack later in the cool of the evening.

She thought that her room was warm, but she staggered back in the sudden heat of the afternoon when she threw open the shutters and looked out across the olive trees in the courtyard to the sea. Outside the air buzzed and the high ground across the water shimmered. The mountains behind it had all but vanished in the haze and looked dream-like and remote. When she had gazed long enough, she pulled the shutters half-shut again and went downstairs.

In the courtyard she found Thea seated at one of the tables in the shade of an olive tree, looking as elegant as she remembered her in her sleeveless blouse and long slim skirt. She and Simon had come to the UK for their honeymoon and to hold a celebration of their marriage for his family and friends, and Thea had looked ethereal and very beautiful.

'You slept well, Zoe? You are rested?'

For a moment Zoe couldn't answer because of being folded in a gentle hug. She laughed as Thea released her. 'Wonderfully rested,' she said. 'I fell asleep almost at once.'

Thea nodded. 'Sit down, please. I will bring cold drinks and food. You are hungry, Zoe?'

'No, really. I think it's the heat. I'd much rather not.'

'You are sure?'

'I'm thirsty, though. I'd love something cool to drink.'

'Then that's what you shall have.'

Above Zoe's head, the olive leaves rustled a little in the faint movement of air. She looked up into the branches, liking the way the trees were spaced, and the tables with their red checked cloths set out at intervals for maximum shade. She noticed that each had metal clips holding the material in place, so perhaps it wasn't always as idyllic as this, although it was hard to imagine.

Thea poured carefully from the jug she had brought into tall frosted glasses and handed one to her. 'Dimitri says you are a good pupil, Zoe,' she said.

'I bought a Greek dictionary and phrase book as soon as I knew I was coming. I shall try really hard, or I won't be much use to you if I can't understand what people are saying.'

'You will be perfect,' Thea said simply.

Zoe felt herself flush. 'I promise to do my very best.'

'Many of our customers are English. They will like to talk to you. And our Greek ones will be pleased to hear you speaking our language.'

'Even though I know so little?'

'They will like it that you are wanting to learn.'

Zoe lifted her glass and took a long drink. It tasted of lemon with a hint of something she didn't recognise. She put her glass down and accepted a square of something sweet-looking from the plate Thea held towards her. 'This looks good. What is it?'

'Baklava. You like it?'

Zoe took a bite and smiled. 'Delicious.' She was surprised to see no evidence of food being prepared for prospective customers.

'Simon will be up soon and then we will be busy,' Thea said as if Zoe had spoken aloud.

Zoe nodded. 'Of course.' Her timing was all wrong. She wasn't at home in Bristol now but was in Elounda for a few weeks, on holiday as Simon had stressed. But she couldn't impose on them like that. There were sure to be plenty of jobs she could do at the Lemoni Taverna that would be helpful, and she liked to feel needed. She wondered if Charles was still at home or setting out on his travels, taking some extended leave from his firm of solicitors and making the most of his freedom and not needing her anymore. The thought was a physical pain.

'You are sad?' Thea's voice was softly sympathetic.

Zoe gave a start and smiled a little guiltily. She had resolved to push thoughts of Charles to the back of her mind, and yet here she was letting them intrude. They had no place in a changed Zoe at the beginning of a different life here — being, she hoped, an asset to the Lemoni. 'Not anymore,' she said. 'Who could be sad in this lovely place? I'm so happy to be here.'

The news of her partial break-up with Charles had spread round the family, and Simon had been the first to offer help in the best way he knew. She had accepted with gratitude, knowing she would be wrapped round with the warmth of his personality. She hoped she would be caught up in his enthusiasm for the life he and Thea had chosen for themselves so that there would be no time to brood. Charles had no idea where she was, so there was no fear of his trying to contact her. She was being as sensible as Charles, and the feeling was good.

She raised her glass and took another sip of the ice-cold lemon. 'This is really delicious.'

Thea looked pleased. 'It's made from our own lemon tree, the one just over there.'

Zoe hadn't noticed the tree before tucked away in a corner slightly away from the others with an area of space around it. She wondered why tables hadn't been placed there but didn't ask.

'Here is Simon now,' Thea said with real pleasure in her voice. She sprang up as he came to where they were sitting.

Yawning, and looking a little dishevelled with sleep, he put his arm round his wife and held her close. 'All right, my little Greek olive?' Then releasing her, he smiled as he sank down on the chair next to her. 'You look puzzled, Zoe,' he said.

'Little Greek olive? That sounds a bit odd.'

'Not a bit of it. The olive is important here. Didn't you know that? Just like Thea.'

Zoe laughed. 'If you say so.'

He grinned too. 'Did Thea tell you that we've a busy evening ahead? One that you'll enjoy, I think, Zoe. Saturday is always special because more visitors have arrived for their holiday on Crete. A lot of them are staying at self-catering places further along the road, and we're the first taverna they come to as they walk into town.'

'And the best,' Thea said.

'Of course.' Zoe smiled at them both.

'Our courtyard is beautiful. They like the tables beneath the olives trees. They like to eat out in the open air.'

'And to gaze at that lovely view?'

Simon looked proud. 'The mountains across the water turn pinkish-mauve as the sun goes down,' he said. 'The afterglow.'

'Sounds magical.'

'That's just what it is, and people like to see it. We start serving early today. About six o'clock or even earlier.'

'And I'm here to help,' Zoe said.

'No way,' Simon said. 'You're here on holiday, Zoe. Thea's family are coming later on, as they do most Saturdays. We sit late into the night. Her brother, Dimitri, brings his bouzouki and plays local music for us. We sing and sometimes we dance while the children play.'

'A party?' Zoe said.

'Not like anything you've seen before,' Simon promised. 'And there will nothing for you to do except to enjoy yourself.'

Thea, nodding, agreed with him. 'The family all help. With the cooking also. We all join in. We have a good time.'

'We certainly do that,' said Simon.

He looked pleased and happy. This was so different from his work as an electrician in Bristol, Zoe thought. That was part of the charm, of course, to make a career of something so different. Brave too. She was proud of him.

'If you're sure I won't be in the way . . . '

Simon's laugh could surely have been heard on the other side of the water. 'You're one of the family too, Zoe. Everyone wants to meet you.'

Part of the family, Zoe thought. That sounded good. She felt welcome and needed and she liked that.

'So, Zoe,' Thea said, 'you must do as you please until then.'

Across the road, the sea sparkled in the sunshine. Zoe looked longingly at it and then made up her mind. 'I'd like to go for a swim,' she said.

3

Floating on her back, Zoe looked up at the bright sky. Not a cloud in sight. Wonderful. This was definitely the life. She closed her eyes and felt herself drift, enjoying every moment after the initial shock. The water had been colder than she has anticipated, and she had hesitated on the edge for a while before taking the plunge. She swam swiftly out to sea until the thin strip of beach vanished behind her. Then she turned and swam slowly back towards the shore to stay in water that now seemed warmer than further out.

Both Simon and Thea had looked surprised at her wish to swim in the sea. 'But it's so cold still,' Simon had said, shuddering.

'Very cold,' Thea agreed.

But this hadn't put Zoe off, because it had looked inviting. Out here in water so clear that she imagined she could count the grains of sand on the sea bed beneath her, it seemed her sad memories of recent events were drifting away. The freedom was exhilarating. But she mustn't stay much longer or she would risk slipping unnoticed through the first early customers in the Lemoni courtyard. She could imagine the scene . . . surprised stares from the guests already seated, others hovering undecided on the threshold and their disgusted expressions as they turned away. No, that wouldn't do.

Hurriedly she waded out of the water, drying herself as well as she could before pulling on her T-shirt over her damp body and slipping her feet into flip-flops. She scrambled up onto the pavement and crossed the road. To her dismay, she arrived at the entrance to the courtyard at the same time as a group of five people hesitating in the entrance. There was no way she could get past them unobserved. Her first thought was to step back into the road and to walk on past the Lemoni in a brisk way as if she had no intention of entering the courtyard but was in a hurry to go somewhere else.

But what was the point of that? She could hardly stride along the road all evening, even though it looked intriguing with its pink paving stones and those lovely shrubs. Goodness knew where she would land up. Taking a deep breath, she followed the others through the entrance and into the shade of the courtyard. Delicious smells wafted across to her. She was hungry now; famished even.

She saw now that the group consisted of an elderly couple with walking sticks, a younger man and two girls who were helping the older ones into chairs with loving care. They had chosen a table near the entrance beneath one of the older olive trees with an uninterrupted view across the calm water to the hills and mountains on the other side. As they settled themselves, they exclaimed with pleasure.

Thea appeared, smiling at Zoe. 'You were back quickly, Zoe. We didn't expect you so soon. Did you enjoy your swim?'

Aware of her wet hair and her damp T-shirt, Zoe felt her face flood with colour. 'It was great,' she murmured.

'Lucky you,' said one of the girls. 'I wish I were out there now instead of here with the old folks.'

'Show some proper respect for your aunt, please, Martha,' the older man said, his eyes twinkling. 'Time enough for swimming when we've eaten. I've a notion it's colder out there than it looks.' He smiled at Zoe. 'Isn't that so, my dear?' He placed his stick by the side of his chair and reached across for the one his wife was using to put beside his.

'I've come prepared for anything,' the girl said. 'Admit you have too, Adam, under those brand-new Chinos of yours. An evening swim. What could be better?'

The young man laughed easily as he

31

leaned back in his seat, not at all put out by the teasing. 'So is this a good place to swim from?' he asked.

He appeared interested; in fact they all did. They seemed a pleasant family pleased with everything. Zoe noticed a strong family likeness between Adam and Martha, the girl who had spoken first. Both had short dark hair, waving a little at the ends, and ready smiles. The other girl was quite different, with her long straight hair and rather gloomy expression.

'It seemed perfect to me,' Zoe said, 'once I was in and had got used to it.'

'Refreshing?' said Adam, his voice sympathetic.

She smiled. 'I could have stayed in for ages, floating on my back and dreaming. Those mountains and the sky getting bluer every moment! It's so beautiful here.'

Thea held out a hand for Zoe's damp towel, smiling too. She looked from one to the other. 'Zoe is here for a holiday at the Lemoni,' she said.

Adam's look-alike, Martha, gazed at Zoe in admiration. 'And you speak English so well!'

Adam flashed Zoe a smile. 'I think you'll find, Martha, that Zoe is speaking her native language.'

'So you're not Greek?'

Martha sounded so disappointed that Zoe was quick to reply. 'It's an easy mistake to make when I've got a Greek name.'

'And a pretty one, too,' the older man said. He looked content, sitting there with his arms on the table as if he were a fixture here for the rest of the evening.

Thea, reminded of her duties, smiled at them all again and left.

'And you are on holiday here?' Zoe said.

'Not all of us,' Martha said. 'Uncle Bill and Aunt Hattie have retired to a place in town.'

'We've been here for nearly a year now,' her aunt said, sounding complacent. 'The best decision we've ever made. But we're always pleased when

33

the family come and bring friends. We've Adam to thank for bringing us over this way this evening. It's a taverna we haven't tried before.'

Zoe looked round at the attractive tables beneath the olive trees and at the earthenware pots of scarlet geraniums brightening a dim corner. 'The Lemoni's run by my brother and his wife now. It's all new to Simon, but Thea's been brought up to it. They're both keen to make a go of it.'

'Then we shall come again, won't we, Bill? Julie's going home next Saturday, but we're sure to come again before then. And the following Tuesday, some good friends are coming to stay. They'll love it here too. And you're here to help your brother and his wife?'

'If they'll let me. But I'm not sure I'm much help.'

'I'm sure you are, my dear.'

This was said so kindly that Zoe was touched. She was tempted to pour out the true reason for her being here but restrained herself. She smiled brightly.

'Thea's family are all coming here later, much later. They do this every so often for a sort of celebration. It gets a bit lively, so Thea said.'

Martha looked at her friend. 'That sounds great, doesn't it, Julie?'

'You'd be welcome to join in if you're still around.'

Thea was back now with a menu in her hand. The moment she had spoken, Zoe regretted the invitation. She had spoken without thinking and was well out of turn. Charles had often warned her to think before she spoke or one day she might land herself in trouble. And now here she was doing it when she had hardly been here five minutes.

She muttered something about being pleased to see them at the Lemoni and that she hoped they would enjoy their meal. Then she went swiftly away, remembering suddenly that since landing at Heraklion she hadn't texted her parents to say that she had arrived safely at the Lemoni, the most attractive taverna in Crete, and that all was well.

Zoe's second shower of the day was a quick one. Dressed afterwards in a cotton skirt and white T-shirt, and with her hair neatly combed and drying, Zoe felt a great deal better. Thea had made no sign she had heard her hasty words, or if she had they hadn't annoyed her. She would hope for the best.

Before going down, she pushed her shutters wide open and leaned out. The air felt cooler now, and for a moment she closed her eyes to enjoy the pleasant movement of the breeze on her face. Charles had often liked to do this, and she had a sudden vision of him leaning out of the window of his flat one evening last winter and gasping as the icy air took him by surprise.

She had laughed and, turning in mock anger, he had grabbed her and pulled her down on the sofa near the window and kissed her so hard her lips felt bruised. Now, shaken by the memory, she opened her eyes quickly and took a long breath. She felt almost as if Charles would be appearing here at the Lemoni for the family party, joining in the fun and being the centre of attention. But Charles didn't know she was here. At least . . . No, it couldn't happen. He hadn't even remembered Simon's name, so how likely would it be that Elounda would mean anything to him?

But thinking like this wouldn't do. What had happened to her resolve to quell thoughts of Charles before they took over and left her a quivering wreck? Making a huge effort, she concentrated on what she could see down below. Through the foliage she glimpsed Thea in her bright clothes, moving serenely among the tables as she welcomed more guests and saw to it that they were seated comfortably.

If she slipped down now, Zoe thought, she would have the chance of apologising for her ill-timed invitation, and at least Thea would be warned. She and Simon had offered her a holiday, and in return she had promised to help them as much as she could. Their enthusiasm was infectious, and she was anxious to be useful, but this wasn't a good start. However, she was doing her best to learn a few words of Greek, and that would show willing. Perhaps with Dimitri's help she would learn a bit more later this evening. The thought of that was cheering.

The sound of children's voices floated up to her: happy at first, and then a shriek followed by cries and an adult voice, angry and threatening. A group of adults about to enter the courtyard hesitated on the threshold. She saw them gesture to each other, turn and move away.

Had Thea seen? She didn't think so. Slightly disturbed, Zoe turned from her window, picked up her Greek dictionary from her bedside table and went downstairs.

4

Darkness fell quite quickly soon after nine, long before Thea's family came bursting in demanding to know why so few customers were here but not waiting for an answer as they dispersed themselves around the courtyard.

Thea had replied to the accusation in rapid Greek, and then turning to Zoe said, 'They just pretend to be astonished. We take no notice.'

Zoe had been unable to translate; but it didn't matter. She only knew that Simon and Thea had seemed pleased about the way the earlier part of the evening had gone and with the part she had played in it, small as it was.

'Well done, Zoe,' Simon had said when the courtyard emptied of customers. 'And you've spoken some Greek too.'

Zoe felt herself flush. Every now and

again she had had a quick glance at her phrase book and had tried to memorise a suitable phrase, but it was difficult. 'I spoke hardly any,' she murmured.

'They liked it. I could tell.'

She smiled. This was encouraging. She couldn't wait to try it on Dimitri. But where was he?

As well as the lights round the edge to illuminate the courtyard, Simon had rigged up coloured ones in the lemon tree area to provide a focal point for Dimitri to sit and play his bouzouki. It all looked charming, with the feathery shadows from the olive trees decorating the tables and the spaces between them.

For some reason, Dimitri was slow to take up his position, and Zoe could see that Simon was becoming impatient as the evening wore on by the way he rubbed his hand across his forehead as he moved between his guests. He greeted each by name and rustled the hair of some of the younger children.

Most of the family were already here,

voluble and pleased to meet the beautiful Zoe, the sister of their dear friend Simon who made their beloved Thea so happy. The children stared at her, wide-eyed, until their parents told them sharply to behave themselves. At least that was what Zoe presumed they said, because the youngsters gave her brilliant smiles and then ran off among their many relations.

At once Zoe was caught up in the friendly atmosphere. It was hard not to feel part of it, with all the lively chat and the surging towards the kitchen area to inspect what Simon had going on there. 'Come in, come in,' he boomed, obviously loving it.

They needed no second invitation — being, Zoe reminded herself, used to taking charge from their years of working here. She stood back for a moment and watched them until an elderly couple she knew were Thea's parents beckoned to her to sit with them at their table. They were both leaning back and obviously enjoying being back in a place that had been home to them for many years.

Thea had told her with pride that they now lived in Agios Nikolaos in their apartment in one of the white buildings overlooking the sea. They had time now to appreciate the beauty of the Gulf of Mirabelle that Zoe had glimpsed only briefly on her way through from the airport. Other family members were from Heraklion, further away still, but enjoying their visits to the Lemoni. Tonight family friends had been invited too, and that was why there were so many of them.

'It is good to meet you,' Thea's father, Yiannis, said. 'Simon speaks kindly of you to us. Welcome to the Lemoni. We are pleased you are here with us. Isn't that right, Anna?'

His wife, as small and attractively plump as her husband, beamed at her. 'We hope you will be happy here with us, Zoe.'

Zoe smiled her thanks. She liked the friendliness of this cheerful pair. Both were dressed in dark colours, but Anna's black dress was brightened by a cream and brown scarf that gave her a decidedly elegant air.

'And now you will tell us more about yourself.'

Usually Zoe found this difficult, but she found talking about her weekends getting together with friends for trips to the theatre and sometimes out walking on the nearby hills was easy. Her university years had been spent in London, but after that she had been lucky enough to get a position in a village school south of the city of Bristol until it was closed down. Since her father had become ill and her mother needed more support, it was best to continue living at home.

'I did just temporary teaching then,' she said, her voice light, 'and then it seemed a good idea to come out to Crete for the summer and help out here at the Limini.'

Yiannis looked his approval and Anna smiled. Zoe was pleased to find that their English was almost as good as their daughter's. This should have been no surprise, considering the business they had run that relied on the tourist trade.

'I'm delighted to be here,' she said, and realised it was true. No regrets, not one. For the moment, anyway, she had almost forgotten the true reason for coming to Crete, and for this evening wouldn't think of it.

Food appeared, brought to their table by two young girls who were obviously fascinated by Zoe and found it difficult to tear themselves away. Laughing, she answered their questions until they were shooed away by Thea's father. 'Away you go, off, off!' With mischievous glances at Zoe, they darting away, giggling.

Although she didn't know quite what she was eating, Zoe found it delicious, and her appreciation pleased both of them. After a while, they were all summoned into the kitchen premises to choose for themselves from a selection of dishes for the next course. It was all exuberance and laughter and a crowding of the surrounding tables that brought a flush to Zoe's cheeks and a brightness to her eyes. She was enjoying herself, and it felt wonderful.

And then Dimitri was there, greeting his parents and smiling at Zoe. The gleam in his dark eyes held warmth that seemed to run through her. That Greek phrase she had learned had vanished and she couldn't recall even one word of it.

'I am late,' he said. 'I had arrangements to make.'

'As late as this?' his father demanded.

'The evening is young.'

Zoe giggled. Dimitri was obviously a law to himself, answering to no one.

His mother smiled fondly up at him. 'You are hungry, my son?'

'I need to eat.'

'Then go. They are waiting for you.'

Zoe watched him vanish into the kitchen region and heard the gale of laughter that greeted him.

45

Anna smiled. 'He's a good boy.'

'I want music,' Yiannis said.

And soon it came. For a moment everything fell silent as the evocative sounds of music rose about the chatter. Zoe listened, enchanted, and even when the talking started again she was hardly aware of anything except for the beauty of the sounds, and the coloured lights casting patterns on Dimitri's face as he swayed with the music he was playing with such abandon.

The children clustered round him, and then some singing began, and three young men leapt to their feet and began to dance, their arms entwined at their shoulders. Others joined in, and when at last the music stopped Zoe noticed that two girls had joined her at the table and were gazing across at Dimitri in wonder.

'Martha,' she cried, recognising her now. 'And . . . '

Martha swung round. 'This is Julie. My friend, Julie.'

'Hi, Julie.'

Zoe hadn't had a chance to tell Thea or Simon she had invited them. But then she saw that it didn't matter because Yiannis had noticed their arrival and was pulling across two extra chairs.

'You are friends of Zoe? Welcome to the Lemoni.'

'Oh . . . thank you.'

Martha flushed a little, but her friend Julie was staring round, obviously impressed by the crush of people.

Anna got to her feet. 'You are doing a kindness by joining us,' she said. 'And now I shall take you to into the kitchen so you can choose what to eat. Don't be afraid. Zoe will come too.'

'Are they always as friendly as this?' Martha whispered to Zoe as they joined the crowd around the array of hot dishes and Anna returned to their table.

Simon came to them, was introduced and greeted them warmly. Zoe was proud of the way he took charge, explaining in great detail what each dish contained and its Greek name. She could see how much all this meant to him and was delighted to be part of it. He was a good man. He had taken her part when she was a little girl and being bullied by one of the boys that lived next door. She had never forgotten that or the other times when Simon had saved her from difficult situations. She owed him a lot.

'It's so hard to choose,' Julie said.

Laughing at her, Simon pointed to the nearest one. 'Try that one. Take just a little; and if you like it, come back for more.'

* * *

The evening wore on and, hypnotised by the music, Zoe felt her eyelids droop until at last she knew that if she didn't take care she would fall asleep at the table.

Yiannis, aware of the situation, smiled at her kindly. 'You are tired, little one? It is time for us to leave.'

Zoe realised suddenly that the music had stopped now and that people were beginning to go. Not only that but

Martha and her friend were over by the lemon tree where Dimitri was standing up and stretching. He looked magnificent in the light from the tree and for a dazed moment Zoe's heart missed a beat. Then she jerked herself properly awake and smiled across at him. He came across at once.

Martha followed him, looking anguished. 'We should have gone home hours ago,' she said. 'It's got so late. We didn't realise.'

'Sorry,' Julie said.

Dimitri put an arm round each of them and smiled his wide appealing smile. 'It was our pleasure to meet you here.'

'We need to settle up.'

By the sudden hush, Zoe knew Julie had said the wrong thing. Stricken, she looked from one to the other, not knowing what to say. But Dimitri bent low over her hand and kissed it in an extravagant gesture that had them all laughing. 'Allow me to drive you home,' he offered.

49

But there was no need. A car drew up on the other side of the wall and Adam was there. His face lit up when he saw his sister and her friend.

'Just in time,' Simon said in a voice tinged with relief.

5

In the days that followed, Zoe found she was settling down to the life much quicker than she could have imagined. She woke early and was out of bed at once, opening her shutters to check that the olive trees in the courtyard were still there, and so was the golden ball of sun rising above the high ground to the east and casting a golden shimmer on the sea.

Every day started off with a swim that was invigorating and enjoyable. On Wednesday morning Simon joined her, looking bronzed and healthy in his swimming shorts, confident that he could leave her far behind. He flexed his muscles as he paused on the edge before taking a running dive. She laughed to see the shock on his face as he surfaced, gasping. In retaliation he set off with his swift crawl, shouting out a challenge to her. Well-practised from her daily stint at the leisure centre at home, she caught up with him with ease.

It was clear that Simon was out of condition when at last he headed for shore and got out wheezing and spluttering. 'Where did you learn to swim like that?' he accused.

Laughing, Zoe told him. She picked up her towel to dry herself. The mountains across on the other side looked hazy this morning, and the sea was as smooth as silk. A tiny boat came out from shore further along, moving purposely through the water towards the open sea. She had seen boats go past later each day, much larger and filled with people, but this one was different. 'Where do you suppose it's going?' she asked.

'Fishing, perhaps. Who knows?'

Zoe towelled her hair and shook it back behind her ears. She loved the way sunshine caressed her skin with warmth even this early in the day.

As they climbed up from the beach onto the road, Simon said, his voice full of doubt, 'You like it here, don't you, Zoe?'

She laughed at him, surprised he could even ask. 'Do I look as if I'm having a miserable time?'

'Well, no,' he conceded. 'It's Thea, that's all. She worries a bit.'

'It's beautiful here, Simon. You know that. And the atmosphere's so laid-back and warm. Friendly people, too, and Thea's so kind.'

Bristol seemed a million miles away. And Charles? Apart from a tiny ache that was often with her, she found she could forget him for hours at a time. It was only in the middle of the night, waking perhaps from some unexpected noise from somewhere far away, that she found herself reliving that last scene and wondering exactly when he had started to have doubts. She still couldn't understand how she hadn't picked up on it straight away.

'You've saved my life by inviting me

out here, you and Thea, Simon.'

He laughed. 'You exaggerate, dear Zoe.'

'Only a little.'

They crossed the road. Even the shade from the olive trees felt warm this morning. There was no one about.

'Sit down and I'll bring us a drink,' Simon said. He spread his towel over the backs of two chairs and took hers from her to do the same with that. Someone had removed the red-checked tablecloths, and the bamboo tables looked attractive with the shadows of the branches decorating them.

This was a pleasant interlude before she helped Thea clear up the kitchen and prepare for the day ahead. Feeling relaxed from her swim, she enjoyed sitting here with Simon drinking ice-cold orange juice this lovely early morning. But soon she must shower and dress in shorts and T-shirt and see what she could find for breakfast. Usually she helped herself to fruit, thick creamy yoghurt and honey and some of Thea's homemade bread. But not yet.

54

She sighed with contentment.

Simon looked at her, still with an anxious expression in his eyes. She knew what he was about to say, but before he could open his mouth she grinned at him. 'Don't say it, Simon, please, or I'll throw something at you.' She looked round for anything suitable but could find nothing but a fork someone had dropped on the ground. She picked it up and brandished it at him.

'You attack my husband?'

She hadn't heard Thea's approach and her quiet words made Zoe jump.

Before she could say anything, Simon's loud laugh rang out. 'We have a virago here, my love.'

Thea looked from one to the other. 'Virago?'

'Someone fierce and nasty.'

She looked bewildered.

'Stop it, Simon,' Zoe said. 'He thinks he's being funny, Thea.'

'You have annoyed her, Simon?'

Zoe smiled. 'Only by being too kind and anxious about me. You spoil me,

55

both of you. But I'm all right, really. I love it here.'

Thea's face cleared. 'I'm so happy for you to love it as we do. Have you eaten yet?'

Zoe leapt up with alacrity. 'I shall do so at once. Simon?'

'Nothing for me,' he said. 'Not yet, anyway. Go and help yourself, Zoe.'

He and Thea were still sitting there when Zoe returned with her bowl of yogurt. She had made coffee and brought that too. She saw that now both were looking solemn, as if they had the weight of the world on their shoulders, but as soon as they saw her they brightened immediately. Slightly concerned, she looked from one to the other. But Thea was smiling now and Simon looked content enough.

He leaned back and stretched his arms above his head. 'I can't believe how exhausted I am after that swim. And yet here's Zoe as fresh as a daisy tucking in as if she's never seen food before.'

'It's delicious,' she said.

He shuddered. 'I can't even raise the effort to go and get changed. It's cash-and-carry day today, Thea. The question is, will I make it?'

She looked at him and shrugged. 'You wish me to go instead? And Zoe will come with me?'

He slapped his thigh. 'The very thing. You're brilliant.'

Zoe smiled as she scraped the last drop of yoghurt from her dish. 'Anything I can do to help, you know that.'

Simon sat up straight. 'It's a real treat going off to the cash-and-carry. You'll see, Zoe. You can take your time, the pair of you. Have lunch somewhere. See something of the countryside.'

It sounded like a day out the way he was talking but Zoe couldn't help wondering exactly what it involved. In her experience, cash-and-carries were on industrial estates somewhere on the edge of big towns. So far she had seen nothing to indicate anything so mundane in this beautiful area.

'The cash-and carry?' Simon said when

57

she asked him. 'Not far from Heraklion. A fair way away but worth it.'

'Forty miles?'

'Something like that. We go about once a fortnight, more often if we've been extra busy. I'm more than happy staying behind this time if you would like to go with Thea since customers are thin on the ground these last few lunchtimes. She'd like that.'

Zoe glanced at her and saw that Thea was smiling. 'How soon do we leave?' She downed the last of her coffee and stood up. 'I won't be long if you want to go at once, Thea.'

Thea got up too with one graceful movement. 'In twenty minutes we will go.'

Zoe was ready in plenty of time, anxious not to keep her waiting. The morning was heating up rapidly, and she was pleased to see that Thea had brought bottles of water, which she placed in the freezer bag on the back seat of the car.

The place was beginning to come to

life as they drove through and up the hill beyond. With the long drive ahead, Zoe settled back in her seat, prepared to enjoy it.

'Soon the place will be filling up as people come for the boats,' Thea said as they gained speed now the town was left behind. 'They go out every day. Have you noticed them? The visitors like to go to the island.'

'The one we can see in the distance near the open sea that's often hazy and interesting-looking?'

'There used to be a leper colony there years ago. Spinalonga. You have heard of it?'

'I think so. The name sounds familiar.'

'In the beginning people with leprosy were sent there to die. A terrible thing. And then after many years a cure was found if they were lucky.'

'Does anyone live there now?' she asked as they reached the turning for Agios Nikolaos. Ignoring it, Thea drove straight on.

'There were about twenty people still

there in 1957 and then they left too. The island wasn't needed anymore.'

'And now?'

'It's a special place. Many people like to visit it. It would be good for you to go there and then you will see.'

'One day,' Zoe said. Thea, she could tell, was flattered at the interest she took in everything they passed and was eager to pass on any information she thought would interest her.

After a while Zoe mentioned Dimitri and how friendly he was.

'Ah yes,' Thea agreed. 'So charming, my brother. We forgive him everything.'

Intrigued, Zoe wanted to ask what they forgave him for but felt it would be too prying to ask. Thea seemed happy to talk and to tell her that Dimitri had backed out of his commitment to the family taverna because he wanted something more from life, something he couldn't properly explain.

'My mother, my father, they were sad but they knew it had to happen. Business was bad, you see. They decided they wouldn't work any longer. They didn't blame Dimitri. No one did.' Although there was sadness in her voice, her mouth turned up at the corners and she gave Zoe a brilliant smile.

'And so that was how you and Simon came to take over the Lemoni?'

'That is so.'

'And Dimitri is happy?'

'He feels free. He likes that. And he paints, oh how he paints. I'll show you. Perhaps today.'

Zoe had a sudden vision of stacks of Dimitri's paintings piled up at the cash-and-carry. An interesting but ridiculous thought.

* * *

Dimitri's studio turned out to be up a long winding mountain road that led far into the hills. The scent of thyme and pure clear warm air hit them as Thea pulled the van up at last in a dusty area just off the road. Up here there was a slight breeze that ruffled her hair but Zoe was glad of the shade of a tree she didn't recognise as Thea indicated she should follow her.

'Just a little walk,' she said.

Being out of the van was pleasant. Laden down as it was after the cash-and-carry visit, the vehicle had made grinding progress up the steep road. As they chugged ever upwards, Thea told Zoe something of her way of life up with here in this barren land where Dimitri was making his home during the week and often at weekends too.

'He said he was tired of people,' she said. 'It surprised us all. And then this place became vacant. You'll see.'

The stone building among a few stunted olive trees looked tiny, but Zoe soon saw that it was bigger than it appeared. At the back was a room the width of the building with wide-open floor-length windows. As they went inside Zoe gazed, entranced at the view of wild mountain scenery stretching far into the distance.

'Dimitri, where are you?' Thea called.

Among the paraphernalia in the room, several easels stood about with half-finished paintings on them that were so colourful that it almost hurt Zoe's eyes to look at them. Then Dimitri emerged from behind one of the easels. There was a moment of startled surprise, and them a beaming smile and a hug first for his sister and then for Zoe.

'You have come to check on me?'

Even though he seemed determined to hide it, Zoe could see that he was delighted to see them, and no wonder living as he did in this deserted place. Alone? It seemed like it from what his sister said.

'We've come to see if you're wasting your time,' Thea said now with a touch of censure in her voice.

His smile was broader than ever. 'I never waste time.'

Zoe moved closer to one of the easels and saw that Dimitri had begun work on a painting of a group of low houses that were startling white against a backdrop of brilliant sea. The scarlet tiles on the rooftops seemed to shine with dazzling light, and she could almost feel the heat of the sun reflecting from them. Suddenly she wanted to go there, to wander round on her own to absorb the atmosphere and the beauty without any distraction and then to return to everyday life a better person because of it.

She felt Dimitri's warm breath on the back of her neck as he came to stand behind her and for a moment didn't know what to say. 'It's brilliant,' she murmured at last.

'A true art lover, this one. She appreciates my work.'

Thea laughed. 'I would too if you ever finished one.'

'To sell for thousands of euros?'

'Why not, Dimitri? They're good, really good.'

She was moving from one to the other as she spoke and then stopped to peer closely at one of them. Zoe could see that this one moved her deeply by the way she stood completely still with her head a little on one side. The painting was of what looked like an abstract work of trees and water and was the only not to feature a building. She saw that Dimitri was watching his sister now, an expression on his face Zoe couldn't quite fathom. For a moment the two of them looked amazingly alike.

Then Dimitri made some facetious remark and the silence was broken. Zoe felt the atmosphere lighten, and when Thea suggested he show them around outside she went gladly with them into the heat of the late morning. She had thought at first that his studio was the only habitation here, and so it was, but there were signs that once there had been others too. When she looked closely she saw crumbling walls half-hidden among the scrub that could only have been the remains of houses.

'A village was here long, long ago,' Dimitri said when she mentioned it. 'Very small.' He held his hands wide apart to show exactly how small, and Zoe smiled. She imagined tiny people in toy-like dwellings moving about their daily tasks, stopping every now and again to peer at the lovely view that to them would seem to go on to the end of the world. 'Would your house have been here then?'

He gave one of his expressive shrugs. 'We do not know. It's old and some of the stone it's built from is the same as the old ones over there.'

Zoe looked across to where he pointed. Now that she was looking more closely, she could discern others almost totally hidden beneath the undergrowth. Once there must have been a thriving community here. It was sad that it was all gone, the people dispersed for whatever reason all those years ago.

'So have you always known your building was here?'

He laughed. 'Questions. So many questions.'

Zoe felt warmth flood her face. Her remark had been an innocent one but it seemed as if there were something deeper here. 'I'm interested, that's all.'

'We found it years ago, my comrade and I,' Dimitri said. 'It was the only one. The room at the back was open to the sky. I saw it had . . . ' He hesitated.

'Potential?'

'Yes, that's it.' He threw her a warm smile. 'Potential. My comrade, he could do these things He put in the glass doors. And then I came here to live and he returned home to his wife. He was happy. His wife was happy. It would have been too lonely for her to live here. She was frightened of the loneliness so far from her people. So I came.'

Zoe looked at him with respect. It sounded so simple. There was no mention of who owned it or the land it stood on. Perhaps these things didn't matter. 'You were lucky then.'

A strange expression flicked across his face and was gone. For moment he had looked furtive, which surprised her. She opened her mouth to say something and then closed it again as he went on to tell her that it was lucky that he could give his friend something he badly wanted.

'A good exchange,' he said with satisfaction.

She would have loved to have known what that was but had the good sense not to ask. She was too curious about other people for her own good sometimes, and it had annoyed Charles more than once.

'You would be interested, Zoe,' Thea said, 'in the ruined Minoan villages. They are ancient. They date back thousands of years. Many people come to Crete to see them. We have so many.'

'One day,' Dimitri said, 'we shall visit one, little Zoe. Together. You will like that?'

'Yes, yes, I will.' She smiled with pleasure. It was great having something so wonderful to look forward to. She hoped it would be soon. Thea looked pleased for her, too. She was a good sister to Dimitri and gave him a warm hug when it was time to leave.

All the way down the mountain road, the warmth of Dimitri's personality seemed still to wrap Zoe round in a glow of confidence. She felt prettier, more certain that in coming out here to Crete was the right thing for her to do.

6

'Simon?' Zoe said as she went into the shady courtyard. For a moment she thought she was alone and then she saw him seated at the corner table.

'We're back.' He looked at her, his face solemn. 'Everything OK?' His voice was flat and uninterested. 'I take it you managed to get everything you wanted?'

She was going to tell him of their interesting visit to Dimitri's new home in the mountains. But no, this was not the right time. Something serious was going on here, and it seemed as if she had no business to enjoy herself away from the Lemoni.

'This isn't like you, Simon,' she said, smiling at him in a way she hoped would lighten his strange mood. Neither was his sitting here when the van needed unloading, but she didn't say so. Thea had driven down the narrow track at the side of the Lemoni and parked at the rear of the building. Even now Thea was clearing a space in the kitchen area for the boxes to be placed for unpacking. She had sent Zoe to find Simon and ask him to help.

'Are you all right, Simon? Can I do anything?'

He stood up with obvious effort and indicated the empty tables. 'I don't know what we're doing wrong.'

'You had no one in for lunch here at the Lemoni?'

'One English couple for coffee, that's all. They looked at the lunch menu and then left. It's been a bad day.'

'But it's not over yet,' Zoe reminded him.

'True, but things don't promise to be much better.'

'You can't know that. We might have a huge crowd in tonight demanding all the lovely Greek stuff Thea's so good at.' She gazed round at the tables with their bright cloths that looked just as fresh and untouched as when she and Thea had set off so cheerfully a few hours ago.

'Where's all that vitality you had only yesterday, Simon?' she said. 'If need be I'll dress up a bit. Or dress down. How about if I go out into the road later in my bikini decked with flowers? That might drag them in. What do you think?'

He laughed. This was better! 'You're ridiculous, Zoe. Won't you ever grow up?'

'I hope not, if it means looking as downcast as you.'

'Just a blip, that's all. Sorry. You do us good being here. Remember that time at Gran's birthday party when we were kids and you dressed up in Aunty Lily's new hat and high heels? I can see the expression on her face now.'

'Nothing wrong with your memory,' Zoe said, relieved to see that his anxious look had gone. 'I was only about five then. I can do better now. Come on, Simon, we need help unloading. Thea will think I've got lost.'

'Ah,' he said as they went inside the dim building and out into the yard beyond. 'I nearly forgot. Those friends of yours, Zoe, turned up wanting to see you.' He greeted Thea with a hug.

Zoe got hold of one of the boxes still in the van and staggered with it to add it to the pile Thea had already unloaded. 'Friends?' she said as she paused, puzzled for a moment. 'Oh yes, the girls who came to the family party.'

'One of them, the smiling one, was wearing a violent yellow top and shorts so brief you could hardly see them.'

Zoe turned a smiling face to him. 'Perfect. Just what we need. That'll be Martha, of course. Did they say what they wanted?'

'They were disappointed not to see you, that's all, especially Martha. The other girl looked a bit glum.'

'And are they coming back?'

'For a meal later on, I hope.'

'There you are, then, some prospective customers. We'll make sure they sit at a table near the front. It'll draw people in. Let's hope the aunt and uncle come too and the brother. A nice little crowd to start things off. What a pity Dimitri can't be here with his bouzouki.'

Simon frowned; but Thea, not noticing, clapped her hands. 'Oh yes. Dimitri would be pleased to see them again. I know it. I shall phone him now.'

'I know it too,' Simon said when Thea had gone in search of her mobile. 'He needs watching, that one. The family don't see it, of course, especially Thea. For them he does no wrong.'

'And for others?'

'That's the question, Zoe. I've seen things . . . '

But Thea was back now, talking excitedly into her phone, a few English words among her rapid Greek. It seemed that Dimitri had started a new painting as soon as they had left him, one that was going to make his fortune. His excitement was obviously spilling out of her phone, infecting his sister with a wild enthusiasm that shone from her eyes and curled her mouth into an expansive smile.

'We need you here, too, Dimitri,' she said in English. 'You might think of coming down to the Lemoni if you finish your work in time?' Thea listened, still smiling, and then switched off and pocketed her mobile. 'That is good,' she said, sounding as satisfied as if she had received a firm promise. Maybe she had, Zoe thought, with a glow of anticipation.

Simon threw Zoe a resigned look and she smiled in response, knowing exactly what he was thinking about Dimitri but refusing to believe it. The work here was now done now and she left them to it, thinking hard.

* * *

Time for a swim ... why not? She wasn't needed here for an hour or two, and both Simon and Thea had made it clear that the afternoon was her own.

Moments later, she crossed the road and jumped down onto the beach. She wasn't alone today. A few families obviously on holiday had taken advantage of the quieter area here further away from town. This was good, of course. They would hopefully notice the Lemoni and consider it for a future visit.

She swam straight out for a while and then turned to float on her back to enjoy the sensation of weightlessness and freedom that always gave her such pleasure. In the distance the Lemoni looked attractive with its wooden arch above the entrance shining white against the foliage of the olive trees. From here she couldn't pick out the tables with their bright tablecloths or the earthenware jars of bright geraniums that stood against the walls, but in her imagination she smelt the subtle scent of the leaves. The place was attractive, and made more so by Thea's smiling welcome. So why were they disappointed by the lack of customers?

She thought of the taverna in the mountain village where they had lunched on their way home. It wasn't half so attractive as the Lemoni, and yet she and Thea had been lucky to find a vacant table there. The noise and chatter must have been heard right across the dusty square. Inside was even noisier when they went in for Thea to greet the proprietors, father and son, whom she had known all her life. It was dim, too, after the brightness outside. Busy as they were, she and Thea were greeted rapturously, and an extra table and chairs were produced at once for them to sit outside in the shade of the building.

They had had to wait a long time for their meal, too, which was disappointingly poor when it came. Even so, it was clear that the people round them were pleased to be there. Everyone appeared to know each other, and even the groups of obvious foreigners like herself were enjoying the atmosphere.

So what was wrong with the Lemoni?

The blue sky above her could give no answer. The sea and the mountains and the harbour were so beautiful that many people from other countries liked to come here. There were many tavernas too. In the mountain village there was no competition as far as Zoe could see. Locals used the only one and welcomed any strangers who arrived into their midst. It was no wonder the atmosphere had felt good.

But the Lemoni was a different place with a different clientele. Here the tourists appeared to predominate, and must be catered for. Most of them came to Crete surely not only for the hot weather but also to experience the Greek way of life. To be somewhere different for a short time and soak up the atmosphere of a place far from home.

* * *

Simon's despondency had completely vanished by the time Martha and her friend arrived at the Lemoni with Martha's aunt and uncle. He greeted them with pleasure and brought the menu to them himself. They were happy to sit in the prominent position beneath the oldest olive tree. Even though Martha had changed from her startling outfit of earlier in the day, she looked eye-catching in her crimson sundress and huge sunglasses.

'Our favourite view across to the mountains,' Bill said with satisfaction as he placed his walking stick at his side and reached across for his wife's. 'Isn't that so, Hattie?'

She nodded and smiled at Zoe. She looked comfortable sitting there in her flowered dress, with a light cream scarf tied loosely round her neck just in case a cold wind started up.

'Tomorrow is Julie's last day,' Martha said. 'So here we are back again.'

'Then that calls for something special.' Simon beamed at her. 'There will be a carafe of wine for you with the compliments of the Lemoni.'

'Really?' Martha was delighted.

Zoe brought it to them and placed it carefully on the table. *Good for Simon,* she thought. *And for business too. Definitely the right idea.*

'Adam ought to be here too,' Julie said. She sounded thoroughly downcast, drooping there at the table as if the end of the world had come.

'We'll see more of him tomorrow,' Martha promised, 'now that he's landed himself a temporary job over on Spinalonga telling groups of people about the place and showing off all the stuff he's been researching.'

'Adam never shows off,' Julie said.

'You're right there, my dear,' Hattie said. 'I expect Adam makes an excellent guide. He's so knowledgeable. I only wish Bill and I could come to hear him too. Perhaps some other day.'

'You'll have to tell us all about it,' Bill said. 'Give him marks out of ten. He'll have earned them, I shouldn't wonder, with all the extra preparation he's putting in this evening.'

Hattie gave a heartfelt sigh. 'I only wish he would consider staying longer with us. I tell him he should have more sense than to leave and go wandering off round the world.'

'Hardly round the world,' Martha said. 'He just wants to see a bit more of it while he has the chance, and I don't blame him. You know what he's like, always on the lookout for more opportunities to come up and hit him.'

Julie scowled. Seeing it, Martha gave a gurgling laugh, looked at Zoe and said, 'Why don't you come with us too, Zoe? We'll be going over on one of the first boats in the morning. It'll be fun.'

'Well, yes, I'd love to but . . . '

'You mean they can't spare you?'

'It's not that.' Of course it wasn't, Zoe thought. Both Simon and Thea had made it clear that she was here on holiday and would be delighted at this invitation. Pleasing them was important, wasn't it? This was a good way of doing just that.

Julie, frowning, glanced briefly at the

menu and made her choice. The others chose, too, and Zoe took their orders into the kitchen. Thea would be pleased that they had all chosen from the Greek menu, Simon too. It could be a good moment to tell them of her plans for tomorrow.

'What would you do if we said no, Zoe?' Simon asked raising both his eyebrows at her so that she laughed and nearly dropped the plate she was holding.

She pretended to consider. 'Play truant? You might not notice I wasn't here.'

'That's true.'

She would have thrown the plate at him if at the moment Thea hadn't appeared in the doorway.

'Some more people are coming now,' she said, flushed with pleasure. 'Look, Simon, Zoe. Five, no six of them. English, of course.'

Simon grinned. 'Don't forget to greet them with *kalispera*, Zoe, and not *kalimera* because it's evening now. *Kalimera* — good day — is for the morning and the early afternoon.'

'Ah.' Zoe, knowing she had already slipped up once or twice, made a mental note to remember this.

'It's a good opportunity to try out your Greek.'

She pulled a face at him. 'Funny!'

'Go on, try it.'

Well, why not? Just a few words, all she knew really, to the set the scene. The Lemoni was a Greek tavern, after all.

'*Kalispera*,' she said when they had seated themselves at the large table in the middle of the courtyard. '*Ti kanete?*'

'We're well, thank you,' one of the younger men said.

'*Melate Ilineka?*'

The girl seated next to him giggled.

'Do we speak Greek? Not so you'd notice, but we're trying hard.'

'Me too,' Zoe said, delighted at the response.

And then they were all laughing and exclaiming and asking Zoe where she came from and what she was doing here. She was pleased to see that another family passing by outside hesitated and then came into the courtyard too.

Thea, busy in the kitchen preparing some of her Greek dishes, was pleased that all three groups were ordering the food she loved to serve. She delighted in making each dish look extra inviting, even though this took a little longer than usual. No one seemed to mind though, and they all sat on through the warm evening as the light began to fade and the mountains across the water looked magical in the afterglow.

7

The water moved gently against the quay as Adam Sanderson, his rucksack slung over one shoulder, stepped into the small motorboat that was to transport him down the shimmering length of the gulf to the island at its mouth for his first assignment as an English guide.

'*Kalimera, Petros. Ti Kanete?*'

The boatman grinned. 'Good day. I'm very well, my friend. Thank you.'

Petros nodded cheerfully as he cast off. Adam settled himself in the bows as he always did when he got the chance. There was plenty of room today with so few people on board. Adam cast about in his mind for something else to say and could only come up with some remarks about the weather.

'*Eena orea mera.*' Hardly original, he thought, but better than nothing and

Petros was pleased at his attempt at conversation, feeble though it was.

'Yes. It's beautiful today. You have risen early?'

'You, too, Petros.'

Petros grinned. 'As always, my friend.'

'Yes, get up early every day,' Adam said in English, smiling too. Petros liked to practise his English just as he did his Greek and was much better at it. 'You have work to do going backwards and forwards to the island with boatloads of tourists. It's only on this trip you use your small boat to take the workers there.'

'That is so,' Petros said, the lines at the side of his eyes deepening as he smiled.

In the pearly haze the island in the distance looked mysterious and full of secrets. Which it was, of course, Adam thought, right from those earliest days when the Minoans were in power. It was at the beginning of the twentieth century that the Greek government designated the island as a refuge for people suffering from leprosy and outcasts from their communities. But now for nearly sixty years the island had been uninhabited, the last of those poor patients gone, cured one hoped of that dreadful disease that once was thought incurable.

He shivered and caught an anxious look from Petros, who stood at the helm looking as calm in his black jeans and sweater as if nothing tragic ever crossed his mind. Adam smiled to show that all was well and then looked back at the harbour with its mountains so close behind he felt he could touch them. A beautiful place that was already beginning to mean more to him than was good for his peace of mind.

They gathered speed and the rising land on either side slid past. Not long now before Petros would be tying up at the jetty on the island and he would spring ashore ready to face his duties. This was his fourth visit, and a feeling of melancholy was always with him when he walked along that cold tunnel the way the condemned men, women and children would be taken when they landed here. It didn't need much imagination to appreciate their anguish as they were led out into mocking sunlight and the sad beauty of the place. The extraordinary thing was that he couldn't keep away and had welcomed the chance to act as a temporary guide.

He took a deep breath and gazed at the land they were passing, trying to pick out the Lemoni Taverna with its olive trees but finding it difficult among the other habitations. He was glad that Martha was bringing Zoe here today.

'Soon more boats will come and you will be busy,' Petros said.

Adam nodded, feeling a tightness in his throat that made him swallow hard. 'I'm fortunate to have the job,' he said. 'The chap who usually does it is ill. That's why. I'm been looking things up, Petros. I hope I remember everything.'

The boatman's grin was broader than ever. 'The people can read. There are information boards.'

'That's what I'm afraid of.' With an effort, Adam smiled too. *Relax*, he told himself. *Even awkward questions can be dealt with. Think of all those possible dangers ahead you might have to face when you move on from Crete.* They didn't give him a moment's concern — wild animals, rough seas to cross, the unknown. A group of interested English tourists wanting information could hardly be compared with that.

Smiling at himself, he stood up as the island came close, ready to jump off and to pretend an optimism he was finding it hard to maintain.

⋆   ⋆   ⋆

Zoe liked the feeling of companionship that being with Martha and Julie provided. They sat on the top deck of the crowded boat, leaning back and soaking up the heat of the day.

'This is the life,' Martha said,

stretching her long legs out in front of her. 'I could travel on like this for ever.'

Julie opened her eyes wide and sat up straight as if she were afraid Martha's wishes would come true. 'Adam will be there already, won't he?' she said, looking anxious.

'He'd better be. He says he'll lose his job if he isn't.'

'And this is his first day?'

'All that studying he's been doing!' Martha sounded disgusted. 'You've seen it him at it, Julie.'

'He's conscientious, that's why.'

'That's right. Stand up for him.'

'Someone's got to.'

Martha moved a little to let a family of small children and their parents squeeze past. 'We're all on holiday here, Julie. Who's going to want a long lecture on the place when it's as hot as this? Not me, for one.'

'I will,' Julie said with determination. 'I want to get the feel of the place and soak up the atmosphere.'

'And you reckon my brother will be

able to help you do that by throwing a lot of facts at you?'

'Yes, oh yes.'

Julie sounded euphoric. Martha laughed, but Zoe felt sorry for Adam having to deal with such high expectations. The pressure would be huge. But what did she know? He might be one of those people who could empathise immediately with his audience and spellbind them with his brilliant descriptions so they hung on to every word.

When he came to the Lemoni with his family on her first day, he had seemed a laid-back sort of person pleased to remain in the background. She could see him now leaning back in his chair and letting the girls chatter on while he took in everything around him. If she had to do his job, she would be tongue-tied and awkward forgetting what she meant to impart half the time until it was too late to do anything about it.

'Rather him than me,' Martha said comfortably. 'I plan to find some shade and spend my time there soaking up the atmosphere. What about you, Zoe?'

Zoe smiled, unwilling to commit herself. 'I'll see when I get there,' she said.

The island was looming up ahead of them now and people moving towards the steps to the lower deck as the boat slowed. On the beach small groups were already forming and as soon as she could Julie headed for the spot where Adam was standing surrounded by several people. Martha, however, hung back.

'I'm going off over there to the shade of that olive tree,' she said. 'That'll do me until it's time to leave.'

Already others had paid the landing fee at the kiosk and were setting off on their own towards the tunnel that they all had to pass through. Zoe glanced at them and then back at Adam and his group. A fleeting expression of alarm crossed his face as he saw them, followed by an uncertain smile.

'I don't think it's a good idea to join

Adam's group, do you?' she said to Martha.

'You're right. He'd be embarrassed with people he knew. Best to leave him alone but try telling Julie that. I didn't even try.'

'You didn't tell me either,' Zoe pointed out.

Martha grinned. 'Not my place to influence you.'

Zoe didn't quite know how to take that, but never mind, Martha meant well. 'Then I'll head off on my own,' she said.

'Adam said you just have to follow the path round the island and you'll end up back here. There's plenty of time.'

'See you then.'

* * *

Adam's group had lingered by the ruins of something that looked to Zoe like a sort of fort and she bypassed it with ease, resolving to return later if there was time to look more closely. There was plenty else for her to see with the shells of various dwellings ahead. Plenty of information boards too, which she paused to read. She learned that the Venetians didn't occupy Crete until the beginning of the thirteenth century and rebuilt the fortress in the sixteenth after the first threat of danger from the Turks. They in their turn ruled Crete from the seventeenth century for about a hundred years.

The solid walls of the deserted hospital further on were impressive, but the church was the greatest surprise as she peeped inside with awe. It looked with its ornate fittings surely just the same as it would have done all those years ago.

On she went until she came to a gap with a sort of slipway leading to the water. Across on the other side she saw the fishing village of Plaka, the nearest place on the mainland looking attractive with its mountain background, beautiful even. But what must the unhappy leprosy victims have felt as they set off in the boat, torn away from family and friends and doomed to die on the island?

She turned away until she stopped again when she reached the seaward side of the island away from the buildings where the water was a deep turquoise and the rocky terrain wilder. She was relieved to be on her own for a few blissful moments. Already she had seen all that she could cope with emotionally on this visit. There was much to absorb and she needed time and space to do it. She would return another day.

She leaned on a piece of jutting-out rock to gaze at the scene before her.

'Great, isn't it?' a passer-by called.

'Lovely,' she said.

Others were coming past now but she was hardly aware of them. Sunlight twinkled across the clear sea and emphasised the deep colour that reminded her painfully of the shirt she had bought Charles just a few weeks ago. He had looked so good in it at his sister's party. And handsome too, with his blond hair falling over his forehead. He had caught hold of her arm so protectively to guide her through the hovering guests to meet his sister. Had he taken the shirt with him on his travels? she wondered. She imagined him folding it carefully and placing it in that navy hold-all of his with part of the zip coming away.

Plunged into further melancholy, she moved on until she rounded a bend and came unexpectedly to a graveyard on the edge of the sea. A lump rose in her throat at the beauty of the place with its backdrop of sapphire water. A good place for the dead to lie until eternity, she thought, but it didn't make up for the drama of human pain. Or did it in some unimaginable way?

She opened the gate and went in. Beneath her feet the ground felt warm and dry even through the soles of her sandals. The ancient tombstones, small and grey, leaned over at strange angles; and one, larger than the rest, had collapsed. She went closer to look, but the lettering had long since disappeared, if there had been any there in the first place. For some reason the sadness of this got to her and she sank down on a mound bare of anything but dry grass.

All at once sheer anger filled her like a mist of swirling red that made her head ache and bitter tears fill her throat. Charles had betrayed her and gone off, uncaring. It had suited him to reject her while he thought things through. And then what? Back she would go at the appointed time to hear his verdict like a docile lamb. His decision. No discussion. What was she doing in a place like this far from home and friends? This enchanted area was mocking her and did nothing to help. A dark, gloomy slum would have suited her better.

At last she rubbed her hands across her face, felt for a tissue and rubbed her eyes hard. All round her the warmth and beauty were still there, and she gazed in wonder to see it. She had agreed to his plan of her own free will, so it was her decision too. She had refused to let him or anyone see how much it hurt. Nothing had changed.

Only then did she see that she was not alone.

'You don't mind me being here?' he said.

'Adam?'

'I saw you when I finished my tour. I thought you might need some help.'

Her lips trembled. 'No, not really. It's . . . kind of you.'

He nodded and sat down too, choosing the fallen tombstone for a seat. He looked relaxed and comfortable as if discovering weeping women was a common occurrence in his daily life.

She took a deep breath, feeling she owed him an explanation. 'It's just . . . well nothing really,' she said. 'I was just thinking of someone, that's all.'

'Someone who made you unhappy?'

'He needed time on his own to work things out, a trial separation. So I came here to Crete. I don't know what he's doing or where he is.'

He registered the bleakness in her voice with concern. 'I take it this wasn't a joint decision?'

She shook her head. 'Not really thought I let him think so. We'd been close for about eight months. I thought . . . you see, it was a bit of a shock.'

Adam said nothing. He was looking thoughtfully at the ground at his feet and she saw that one of the laces on his trainers had broken and was knotted together to make it usable. She wondered what the Greek for shoelace was and if he knew it.

Most people would have said something like time passing or that being in a different environment was bound to help. Because he didn't, she felt his understanding more keenly and was grateful. She looked at the ground too and saw that what she had thought of as a dry twig was twitching slightly. Then, without warning, it shot across a patch of dry earth as if it knew exactly where it was going and wasn't going to vary from its planned route, however many people were watching.

'A lizard,' he said. 'Fascinating, isn't it?'

'You're interested in natural history?'

'That and other things. That's why I want to travel, visit places I've never been before, faraway places.'

'Faraway,' she murmured. 'That sounds scary.'

'Not when you get there. Those places aren't far away then because you're there. It's home that's far away.'

She smiled. 'That's one way of looking at it. Home seems a long way away from where we are now.'

'Bristol, isn't it? I was at university there.' He saw her eyes light up briefly and hastened to talk of the course he had taken and of how the field work was so interesting that it had inspired him in his plans to see what he could of the world while he had the opportunity.

'And is that why you're here?' Zoe said.

'My aunt and uncle wanted me to

come for a few weeks while Martha was on holiday. It seemed a good idea, and now I know it was.'

He was looking at her in such a shy way that she was charmed. She couldn't help liking him. He would make anyone a good friend. 'You travel on your own?'

He smiled. 'The best way.' He stood up. 'I think we should make a move.'

She got up too and glanced hurriedly at her watch. 'I'll be late for the boat.'

'We're not far away. Don't worry. A bit further round the bend and we'll see it coming.'

He stood aside to let her go first through the gate and she saw that he was right. Crowds were gathering on the beach, and Martha had been joined by others beneath her olive tree. Julie wasn't there unless she was lurking behind other people, but Zoe didn't have time to notice before their boat drew up at the jetty and there was a rush to board for the return journey.

8

Zoe had looked forward to this, but somehow the anticipation had gone and she was left with a feeling of anticlimax. She joined Martha on the top deck.

'Julie not here?' she said.

Martha stretched languorously. 'We were going to have lunch when we got back. D'you know the taverna with the bit sticking out into the water? We booked a table right on the end.'

'The Papia?'

'That one.'

'Sounds good.

'We like watching the little fish scuttling about, hundreds of them, and that table's the best one for doing that.'

'But what about Julie? She's obviously missed the boat. Should we be worried?'

'Not a bit. She can look after herself. Missed it deliberately, I expect. She'll be all right. Come and join me, Zoe. Please? I don't like eating alone.'

'You could wait for her. I don't suppose they'd mind.'

'No way. I'm starving.' Martha looked mischievous. 'She might be a long time yet, you know. She can find us later if we're still there. You look as if you could do with a bit of cheering up.'

Zoe hesitated. She glanced back at the island fast fading into the distance. Of course it was as Martha said. No one would miss the boat if it wasn't intentional, but why didn't Julie tell Martha of her plans? Maybe, though, it was a last-minute decision and she wanted to see more of the place.

Martha's smile didn't falter. 'You'll come?'

'Just try to stop me.'

The journey was faster on the way back, as if the boatman was starving too. They stepped out onto the quayside, feeling the heat strike them as they mingled with crowd. The shade from the canopy at the Papia was welcome, and they settled themselves at the table on the water's edge with relief.

'There they are, our friendly little fish,' Martha exclaimed in delight. 'Look, Zoe, down there. Can you see them?'

Zoe watched the tiny fish darting about in the sparkling water. This fish-spotting was something the Lemoni lacked, she thought, but there were other things in its favour that people appreciated. The shade from the olive trees for one, and the feeling of leisured seclusion in quiet surroundings. The warm welcome was the same as here, though, and the bringing of the menu almost as soon as they had seated themselves.

'Now,' said Martha when they had made their choice, 'tell me why you look so sad.'

'Do I?'

'I can see you are. It's that island history, isn't it? I shouldn't have asked to you to come with us.'

'No, it's not that.'

'No?'

The sympathy in Martha's eyes and was almost too much for Zoe. Physically Martha was like her brother, but Zoe had thought they were complete opposites in temperament. Now she could see that that Martha hid her sensitivity beneath a brash way of behaviour that made her seem more confident and uncaring than she was.

Zoe glanced down at the tiny fish again and then at some more people arriving at the Papia. They hesitated for a moment, and then the waiter approached and showed them to the only vacant table nearby. She froze.

'Zoe?'

Zoe started at the alarm in Martha's voice. She looked away from the newcomers, seeing only vaguely a crowded boat approaching the quayside further along before glancing back again. Charles? No, no, it couldn't be. Yet the fair hair was the same, with a lock falling over his forehead. And the way he sat, with one shoulder slightly lower than the other . . .

'It's just . . . just . . . '

'Something wrong? You've gone really pale.'

With an effort, Zoe smiled. She could see now that the man was older than Charles and the woman with him was obviously his wife. And there were children too, a boy and a girl demanding attention as they made a grab for the menu. But the likeness was uncanny. It was hard not to stare.

'It's all right. Really.' Zoe's shock was fading a little now. Poor man, being stared at in that way. Luckily he hadn't noticed, but she suspected that his wife might have.

The half-carafe of red wine they had ordered arrived at that moment, followed by large plates of moussaka and separate dishes of Greek salad. Zoe concentrated on thanking the waiter in Greek and listening to his reply. His smile of appreciation made her smile too, and for a moment she forgot the Charles look-alike seated a short distance away trying to control his children. Then she looked furtively at him again. She knew this man wasn't Charles but at the same time could hardly believe it.

Martha poured wine and then picked up her knife and fork. 'Mmn. Delicious.'

But Zoe was no longer hungry. She made a play of eating; but Martha, frowning, had obviously noticed.

'Sorry, Martha,' Zoe said, laying down her knife and fork.

'Something *is* wrong?'

Zoe moved her chair a fraction in the vain hope that she was out of eyesight of the other table. 'It suddenly got to me over there on the island,' she murmured. 'I thought I was all right, being here and doing all I could to help Simon and Thea. But back there I felt I was suddenly back home again learning that things were terribly wrong between Charles and myself and he didn't want me anymore. We were so close, you see, and talking of marriage.'

'You were actually engaged?'

'It hadn't quite come to that. And then he said he wanted us to have a two-month separation to think things through and I . . . well, I agreed.'

'And now you think it was a bad idea?'

'He said we needed to think things through, to be quite sure how we felt about each other.' Zoe shivered, appalled at the bitter tone in her voice she simply couldn't control. She took a deep breath.

'Sure? Sure of what? That he thinks he can mess you about for two whole months? That's crazy.'

'No, no. He didn't think that. I'm sure he didn't. He was being sensible for both of us. I could even see his point.'

Martha's eyes widened. 'Has he tried to get in touch with you?'

Zoe shook her head. I lost my phone and had to get another one. New number, you see. I made Mum and Dad promise to keep my whereabouts a secret.'

'But won't he guess? I take it he knows you're living here?'

'Crete's a big island. I'm fairly sure

he doesn't know exactly where Simon lives. I don't think it will occur to him that I might join him.'

'Why not?'

Zoe hesitated. She couldn't quite explain that, even to herself. She had assumed that Charles would think she might visit one of her old friends from school, or even just stay where she was. He had never liked the thought of foreign travel anyway. In any case, he would most likely stick with their two-month agreement.

'What happens at the end of the eight weeks?' Martha demanded.

'I shall go home and we'll meet and discuss our relationship.'

'Ha!'

Zoe felt herself flush at the wealth of meaning in that one word. She couldn't help another glance at the other table but then quickly averted her eyes on seeing the little girl staring back at her.

'Well you're here now,' Martha said as if that ended the matter. 'Make the most of it, Zoe. Have a good time. Live a little. And what's more, I shall see to it that you do.'

'And how are you going to do that?'

'How much time do you have off?'

'Afternoons are free. And so are mornings if I want them.'

'There you are then. No excuse. Have you been to Agios Nikolaos yet?'

When Zoe admitted that she hadn't, Martha was full of plans. By the time they had finished this course and had decided on a platter of mixed fruit to share for the next one, Zoe's spirits rose a little.

Martha, leaning back when they had each made their selection, now had an air of complacency about her. 'Even if I can't have the car, Uncle Bill will give us a lift to Ag Nik any time we want. So how about Monday? Be prepared to be picked up from the Lemoni about ten o'clock. Okay with you?'

Zoe smiled when Martha didn't wait for a reply. She was intent on fish-spotting again and was so engrossed that she didn't notice Julie slipping past with her face averted. Zoe was about to call to her but then thought better of it. What was going on between Martha and her friend was no concern of hers. When at last they got up to go, she walked by the other tables without glancing at the one that had so intrigued her such a short time ago.

As they passed the colourful boats unloading their passengers on the quayside, she felt again some of the humiliation of her last meeting with Charles. And now she had seen him, or thought she had. She had struggled to put all these memories behind her and would continue to do so. She had appreciated an interesting boat trip to the island. Not only that, but she was with people who had wanted her with them. Martha, anyway. She wasn't too sure about Julie.

Smiling, she strode out, anxious now to be welcomed back in a place she had come to love.

★ ★ ★

'Your friend was here,' Simon said as soon as she came through the gap into the shady courtyard. He was sitting alone at one of the inside tables from where he couldn't be seen by passers-by. Thea was nowhere to be seen, resting no doubt, as Simon would normally have been at this time of day.

'Friend?' Zoe was surprised.

'The girl, Julie. She looked a bit furtive.'

She looked at him in astonishment. 'But she came with us to Spinalonga. Oh, yes. I remember. She wasn't on our boat coming back.'

'You didn't suggest it then?'

'You're not making a lot of sense, Simon.'

'We need a drink. Wait here. I'll get it.'

Zoe sank down at the table, glad of the shade. Simon came back with a jug of fresh orange juice and two long glasses. There was the tinkle of ice as he poured.

She took a long, satisfying drink. 'That was good. I needed that.'

'But you had a good time?'

'Excellent. We lunched at the Papia. Martha invited me. It gave me a chance to see the opposition.'

'Were they busy?'

'Well, yes. People coming off the boats, I expect. And you?'

She knew the answer from his downcast expression. If she had her way, she would force them all to come out here from the centre of town. It was an attractive walk along the path by the water with the oleander bushes and the shady trees.

He shrugged. 'One couple, that's all, and they didn't want much. Julie could see how it was.'

'She didn't eat here?'

'Perhaps I should have offered her something as a consolation.'

'For what, Simon?'

'There just isn't the work, you see. And I thought you told her there might be so I felt a bit awkward.'

'She wanted a job here?'

'She'd do anything, she said.'

'But that's odd. She's supposed to be leaving tomorrow.'

He sat up straight and smiled, obviously relieved that he had got it wrong. 'Well it can't be helped. We don't need more staff and I told her so.'

He took a long drink and put his empty glass down.

'I gather she was after some accommodation too. You see how busy the town is, Zoe. Everything booked up I shouldn't wonder. I wouldn't like to be in her shoes.'

Zoe wouldn't either. But if the Lemoni's trade didn't pick up very soon she might well be in the same position herself.

9

In town next morning Zoe emerged from the post office into the heat and noise of the busy street and then stopped suddenly, causing to person behind her to leap out of the way. She turned quickly.

'I'm sorry,' she said in English and then in Greek '*Signomee* . . . '

His deep, throaty laugh was familiar and so was his mock bow. 'Dimitri?' For a moment she thought she was greeting the wrong person as she saw the single rose in his hand. Against his tanned flesh, the bloom was a delicate pink and looked so out of place that she hesitated. 'Oh, I . . . '

He held the flower out to her, and Zoe took it and held it protectively against her in case a hurrying passer-by should injure it.

'I haven't seen a rose like this for ages.'

'You like it?'

'It's beautiful.'

Once the rose was her favourite flower, especially scented ones like this that grew in Charles' sister's garden. She had plucked one from the overhead arch and given it to him and he had held it cupped in his hand. If he had kept it, the petals would be dried and withered now and the scent gone.

She glanced up at Dimitri and smiled. His curly hair looked wilder than ever and his eyes shone with delight at her pleasure in the perfect bloom. 'Come, Zoe. It's quieter further on, and I have something to show you.'

She went with him gladly, the traffic noise getting to her now in a way she hadn't really registered before. Some shade would be welcome too. Already the petals of the rose seemed to droop, and she didn't want that.

'So where did you get the rose, Dimitri?' she said.

'There is one place near here that grows an English rose bush. I think we

116

will go there one day.'

'And why did you pick it, Dimitri?'

Grinning, he shrugged.

Intriguing. But that's how Dimitri liked to be. He would tell her in his own good time. Meanwhile, it didn't matter. He was hustling her along and she liked the feel of his warm hand on her bare arm.

An open sports car was parked where two roads converged, one leading out of town and the other going steeply downhill towards the glittering water. That this wasn't a good place to leave the vehicle didn't seem to bother Dimitri. He let go of her and put his hand instead on the shiny red car, beaming with pride.

She smiled. 'Yours?'

'Jump in, Zoe.'

She slid into the passenger seat and placed her precious rose in the narrow aperture in the dashboard that seemed made for it. 'Now I'll show you how she goes,' he said.

Fast, as it turned out as they swept

down the road to the causeway and across to hilly land on the other side.

'Where are we going?'

He laughed, throwing his head back in the gesture that was pure Dimitri. 'You will see, little one.'

They were on a narrow-rutted track now winding uphill. The wind in her hair was bracing and she laughed with the joy of it. Knowing that Dimitri wanted her with him was great even if it was only to show off his new possession.

The beach he took her to was on the far side of the hill and looked invitingly out to sea. He parked the car and they walked down a steep path to where the sand was silvery gold and sunlight danced on the clear water. No man-made beach this but one as beautiful as nature could make it.

Zoe sighed with pleasure and hearing it Dimitri took her hand and raised it to his lips. Then he let it go and laughed.

'I came here as a boy,' he said. 'Often alone. Sometimes with friends. We made a promise, a pact I think you say. All of us.'

She wanted to ask what it was, but something in his expression stopped her. He was looking out to sea now, a slight frown indicating that he was deep in thought and for a moment had forgotten her. Then suddenly he brightened and his smile was as warm as ever.

They began to walk. The beach was a small one, bordered on each side by areas of rocks shining white in the sunshine. She would have liked to linger for a while to enjoy the view of sea and mountains. Here was a magic place, a place where you could feel the worries and anxieties of everyday seep away in the gentle breeze. Humiliating memories too, she thought with wonder. It was freeing and wonderful in a way that made her aware of her surroundings in a deeper and more meaningful way.

'You are sad, *koucala*?' Dimitri said with concern.

She smiled. 'Sad? Oh no. In this enchanted place how can I be sad?'

For an answer he put his arm round her and pulled her close. His kiss, when it came, was surprisingly gentle, so that her first involuntary attempt to pull away seemed ridiculous. She relaxed as he kissed her again, longer this time.

'A beautiful girl in a beautiful place,' he murmured as he released her. 'And now I too have broken the pact.'

She gazed at him, her heart full.

'Too?' she said.

He frowned. 'My friends and I . . . our pact was sacred. I thought so, I believed so.'

'But it wasn't?'

'I have been told something about one of us I do not like.' He indicated the rocks at the right-hand side of the beach. 'Come. We go. There is another place round there.'

'Better than this one?'

His shoes were off in now and she bent to undo the straps of her sandals too.

'Very soon I think we will see something I need to know.' He finished rolling up the legs of his jeans and took her by the hand. 'Come.'

The water was icy but he didn't seem to feel it and was knee-deep as they rounded the rocks. Ahead of them she saw a wooden jetty, stark and very new. She turned to Dimitri in surprise.

His face looked grim but he said nothing as they paddled out of the water onto the warm sand.

'This is what you have come to see?'

'To inspect it, yes.'

He didn't move from where they were standing but glanced at his watch, frowning again. He seemed far away, intent on something on the horizon, his body rigid. Then suddenly he relaxed. She could see now that a vessel was coming towards them, small at first and then larger as it came closer. Soon she saw that it was like one of the craft she often saw passing the Lemoni crowded with holidaymakers. It slowed down as it approached the beach and eased its way gently to the jetty. From Dimitri's swift intake of breath she knew that this was what he had come to see.

People were beginning to disembark now, helped by someone whose presence obviously angered Dimitri. He watched for only a moment and then grabbed Zoe's hand so hard she cried out in pain. 'We go. Now!'

She saw that there was a narrow path away from this beach too, so there was no need to paddle back round the rocks. In any case, the first beach wouldn't be secluded for long. Already some of the passengers were making their way there, spreading out across the area, talking and laughing.

'We promised,' Dimitri said through gritted teeth. 'We made a pact not to bring others here. And now this!'

She said nothing as they went swiftly up the path that was so narrow in places she had to fall behind. His reaction was hard to understand. He had done the same by bringing her, a stranger, to this place. There was beauty here that many would appreciate, and it could never be hidden for long. In any case, Dimitri and his friends had been boys when they came here long ago and made the secret pact between them. The passing years were bound to bring changes in outlook as they matured. Surely he could understand that.

She looked at him thoughtfully. Dimitri was a complex character, and she hadn't suspected that he was more than a charming, generous man who lived life to the full. But beneath the surface was someone who bore grudges, who lashed out in fury on occasion. Perhaps beneath everyone there was something else that not everyone saw? She had assumed she knew Charles well and then discovered she was mistaken. Now, she blamed herself for being unable to understand how things stood with him just as Dimitri should understand that there must be change as the years passed.

In his fury he seemed to have forgotten this, but when they reached his car she saw that his smile when he looked at her was warm again.

'I was angry,' he said. He looked so

repentant that her heart was touched.

'But not with me?'

'No, oh no. Never with you.' He opened the passenger door for her and then leapt nimbly over into his own seat.

He had driven fast on the way here but it was nothing to the speed he took the track down to the road to the causeway. Zoe held on, hoping he'd have the sense to slow down through the narrow streets of the town when they got there.

Dimitri's spirits seemed to sink even lower again when they got there, probably because of the hold-ups waiting for them as they joined the stream of traffic where the two roads met. His hands clenched the steering wheel and his frown deepened. The Greek he was muttering to himself left Zoe in no doubt that it was a good thing she couldn't understand what he was saying. She sank lower in her seat.

They crept forward.

'Hi, Dimitri, room for a little one?'

The English words were called out to him in a voice Zoe recognised. Surprised, she shot upright as they drew to another halt.

Dimitri turned his head too. 'Julie?'

'Dimitri, I stayed. I didn't go home.' She was gazing at Dimitri in a way that suggested something more than casual friendship. He, too, seemed delighted.

The car ahead of them began to move, and the stridency of the horn of the one behind sounded impatient. Slowly they inched forward with Julie walking beside them. Zoe hadn't seen her so animated before. She smiled and chattered to Dimitri until she realised, with a suddenness that changed her expression to one of shock, that Zoe was seated in the car beside him.

Dimitri, though, was undaunted by the possessive way Julie's hand clamped down on the door rim.

More hooting from behind and shouts too. Unconcerned, Dimitri gave a friendly wave and then indicated that he was pulling into the parking space on the other side of the road that had just this minute become vacant.

Zoe put her hand on the door intending to get out, but he leaned across and covered it with his own. 'Wait, little one. We have room for three.'

'No, no, this is fine, Dimitri, really.'

'The day is young. We have places to go.'

Aware of Julie's glaring reaction, she shook her head. She had some thinking to do and wanted space on her own to do it.

'I'll be needed at the Lemoni,' she said, 'but thanks, Dimitri. That was a wonderful place. Thank you for taking me there. We'll be seeing you later?'

His face lit up into a pleasant smile. 'I shall be there. My bouzouki too. My sister is expecting me and now you too, my little *koucala*.'

'*Koucala*?' Zoe heard Julie ask as she walked away, followed by Dimitri's deep laugh. 'What does that mean?'

She didn't look back as she joined

the path skirting the colourful boats in the harbour. She had to face the suspicion that she always took things at face value and didn't find it easy to do otherwise. What a thing to admit, even to oneself! The knowledge was humbling.

It wasn't until she was in the coolness of the grove of trees further along that she realised that her precious rose lay discarded in Dimitri's car.

10

Martha turned up alone at the Lemoni that evening because her aunt and uncle had been visiting friends all day and were tired. Exhaustion probably applied to Adam too, Zoe thought. What was unusual was Martha's worried expression and the way she didn't glance at the menu in her usual exuberant fashion but pushed it away when Zoe handed it to her.

'I'm not really hungry, Zoe. Sorry. I just wanted to see you to tell you that Julie's got a job at that taverna, the one on the corner near the church. She's not going home.'

'The Rosebowl?'

'Stupid name.'

'I saw her earlier, very briefly. A bit of a surprise. D'you know why?'

Martha gave a little shrug. 'She loves the place apparently, but don't we all?

She's emailed her boss back home to say she's not coming back. Aunt Hattie's beside herself. Says she feels responsible for her as her guest and worried that Julie's mum and dad will blame her.'

'But that's nonsense.'

'Of course it is. But she's feeling guilty because her friends are coming to stay on Tuesday and there's no more room. Poor Aunt Hattie.'

'And your uncle?'

For a second Martha's eyes lit up. 'He tells her not to be an old fool. But I can see he's concerned too.'

Zoe thought of that kind couple, Martha's aunt and Uncle, who were in an impossible situation. 'But suppose Julie can't find anywhere else to stay?' she said.

'She says she's got contacts but she won't tell me anymore than that. I don't know what's got into her.'

Martha's voice died away and she looked so woebegone that Zoe wished she could stay with her for longer instead of needing to welcome the family of three who had just come hesitantly into the courtyard. They had arrived in Elounda only recently, they told her, and needed a quick snack before settling into the holiday complex further along the road.

By the time Zoe seated them and helped them choose something that Simon could produce quickly, Martha had got up to leave. 'Is it still on for Ag Nik on Monday morning?' she said.

'Of course. But you'll be back later to the family party later as my guest, won't you? My turn to cheer you up, Martha. Please?'

'Maybe.' Martha didn't sound too sure. She pushed her chair beneath the table as if it was the most important thing in the world to leave the place as tidy as she had found it.

Zoe watched her, frowning, trying to think of something that would attract her. 'Dimitri's promised to come. There'll be music.'

'Are you trying to tempt me?'

'That's the idea.'

'Mmn. Not sure that's good enough. He's not my favourite man.'

Zoe was surprised. 'You don't like him?'

'I wouldn't put it quite as strongly as that. There's something secretive about him that seems odd, that's all.'

Zoe thought briefly of Dimitri's glowing personality and his obvious popularity. But not with everyone, it seemed. She would think about that. 'Please come, Martha,' she said. 'We'll get a chance then to talk properly.'

Suddenly Martha smiled. 'Maybe. But be warned. Julie says she's been invited too if she can get away in time. She's determined to stick around.'

'I see.' But Zoe didn't. Who could have invited Julie? Not Simon or Thea for sure.

She watched Martha pick up her bag and head off through the gap and across the road. Dusk was already falling, and the light on the distant mountains was beautiful.

She watched until Martha was out of sight and then turned back to her duties, ready to welcome more hopeful customers but not at all certain there would be any.

*　*　*

For some reason the atmosphere at the family party was different this time. Some of the children were quarrelsome and needed stern words from their grandfather to make them behave. The parents of one of the little ones took exception to this and needed placating by their grandmother, Anna, who for once hadn't seemed quite like her indulgent self.

Zoe's initial disappointment at Martha's absence soon faded when she saw how it was going to be. This wasn't the atmosphere to cheer anyone. Not only that, but she was kept busy pacifying one little boy who clearly thought he would have a better time somewhere else.

When at last Dimitri came, his arrival was greeted with joy and relief, but even he had seemed subdued and the music he played not quite as lively as usual. He hadn't once glanced at her when he arrived. There seemed no reason for Dimitri's odd humour unless she was missing something. The food was excellent and there was plenty of it. But Dimitri had waved his hand in a dismissive way that Zoe could see upset Thea who looked at her brother in concern.

'You are unwell, Dimitri?'

He shrugged. 'I have eaten at Niko and Agneta's house. We had much to discuss.'

'And it made you ill?'

Shrugging again, he turned his back on her. Simon, unaware of this exchange, was busy clearing the space beneath the lemon tree and seeing to it that a chair was placed in exactly the way that Dimitri liked it.

'There,' he said, beaming at his brother-in-law. 'Perfect, or what?'

Before Dimitri could answer, there was a slight disturbance as his mother, perhaps picking up on something unusual in the atmosphere, had rushed towards him and given him a huge hug. 'My son!' she cried, her voice muffled against his shoulder.

He was still for a moment, holding her, glancing behind her at the old olive trees on the land next door with an inscrutable expression on his handsome face. Then she broke away and gazed up at him.

'*Meetera*,' he said, his tone even. 'I have come to play my bouzouki.'

'But we haven't seen you for days. Have you no words for your father, for me?'

It seemed he hadn't, for he turned away; and his eyes, meeting Zoe's, had some indefinable expression in them. She was aware of an obscure uneasiness and looked over his shoulder at the motionless olive trees that had seemed to draw his attention moments before. Then he caught sight of Julie coming towards him, drooping a little with obvious exhaustion but with a wide smile on her face.

'I'm staying in Elounda, Dimitri,' she said in triumph. 'I've found a job.'

His face lit up. 'You have work? Here at the Lemoni?'

'Not here. At the Rosebowl. Isn't that great? For the whole summer if I can find somewhere to stay.'

His smile faded. 'At the Rosebowl, that place? But you have nowhere to live?'

'Not after Tuesday. I'll find somewhere.'

'In town there is nowhere. I know it. Niko knows it. He was telling me. All accommodation taken.'

He sounded concerned. Too concerned, Zoe thought. Thea seemed to think so too, judging from her expression as she moved to one of the tables to pick up a pile of empty dishes.

Dimitri said nothing more as he sat down and picked up his bouzouki. At first the tunes were cheerful, but then he changed to another that had a mournful ring to it as he looked again at that spare piece of land.

After that Zoe was busy collecting empty dishes to carry out to the kitchen where Thea had made a start on the washing up. She crashed a dish down on the draining board so hard it almost bounced off. This was so unlike her that Zoe was alarmed. 'Thea? You're unwell?'

'Not that.' She rubbed one dripping hand across her face. 'I know what will happen,' she said. 'I know my brother. He will be deceived by that girl. He will suffer.'

'You really think so?'

Tears filled Thea's eyes and her lips trembled. This was bad, really bad. Zoe didn't know what to do. She looked round despairingly, but there was no help in the piles of dishes and the tea towels hanging on the rail above the table. There was a box of tissues on the shelf near her, and she grabbed it and pulled some out.

'Oh Thea,' she said, holding them out

to her. 'I wish I could help.'

Thea was in floods of tears now, and Zoe pulled a chair forward for her. Thea sank down in it and for a moment sat with her head in her hands. Then she looked up and grabbed a tea towel and rubbed at her face.

'I'm not ill, dear Zoe,' she said. 'I feel strange, that's all.'

'I'll get Simon.'

'*Ochi*. No. Do not tell Simon. He will be angry that Dimitri upsets me.'

'But surely you don't think Dimitri will invite Julie to stay at his place?'

'He has empty rooms. She needs somewhere to live.'

'But his place is up in the mountains, miles from anywhere.'

'He will drive her down each day. You will see. He will arrange it.'

She sounded so sure that Zoe was almost convinced. 'But what about his paintings?'

Thea gave a deep sigh as she struggled to her feet. Her white face alarmed Zoe, but she made no attempt to restrain Thea as she reached for the dishcloth and plunged it into the sink.

'He will no longer work,' Thea said with her back to Zoe. 'She will stop my brother from doing the work he left here to do. In Aghios Nikolaos there is a gallery, an important one by the sea where the tourists like to go. They have agreed to take his paintings if he does enough of them. He needs them to show his work. It's important. But he tells me nothing.'

Zoe thought of the beautiful half-finished work she had seen on the easels in Dimitri's studio and his enthusiasm for glowing colours and brilliant strong strokes. Surely he wouldn't forgo this opportunity the gallery was giving him?

* * *

Zoe's swim next morning was brief. Somehow the feel of water on her warm skin did nothing to inspire her to strike out swiftly from shore as on other mornings. The lateness of getting to bed last night must be to blame. There had been more clearing up to do last night than usual because Thea, desperately exhausted, had been forced to go upstairs. Knowing that she always liked to get the place straight at once and not leave it until the morning, Zoe had done what was needed before heading off for bed herself.

She swam only a little way before she turned to float on her back. But the peace and tranquillity of the early morning were swamped by the thoughts of last evening and of Dimitri's strange mood. At soon as she arrived, Julie had sunk down on a nearby chair and leaned confidentially towards him, and it was obvious that he liked her near him. As the evening drew on and people started to depart, Julie had made no effort to move.

For once Dimitri's parents were the last to leave; and just as they had concluded their emotional farewells, a car drew up outside. As Adam appeared through the gap into the courtyard, Zoe saw Julie's look of alarm.

'Julie, your lift is here,' Simon called.

Adam smiled at Zoe as he came forward, looking in his blue open-necked shirt relaxed and happy to be here. Simon moved forward to greet him.

'Just in time for a nightcap. You'll join me in something, Adam?'

'Afraid not, but thanks. Another time perhaps, when I'm not driving. Did the evening go well?'

There was a moment's silence, and then Julie sprang up. 'A good time was had by all.' Her voice sounded more high-pitched than usual. 'Isn't that what they always say?' She looked round for confirmation. 'Let's get going then, Adam, if you insist. We're finished here.'

There was a sudden commotion as a chair went flying. The next moment Thea lay in a crumpled heap on the ground. Simon let out a strangled cry and was immediately down at her side.

'I'm all right,' Thea had gasped as she tried to sit up. 'I'm tired, that is all. Please, I will go to bed.'

The next few moments were a blur of

exclamations and advice, but somehow Zoe and Simon between them had helped Thea up to their room, and when she came down again everyone had gone. She had taken her time with the clearing up, glancing up every now and again at Simon and Thea's bedroom widow, where no light gleamed behind the shutters.

They were still closed this morning, so it looked as if Thea was having a lie-in, and that was good.

11

'So tell me all,' Martha said as she and Zoe leaned on the warm railings that edged one of the three waterfronts of Aghios Nikolaos next day. They had just waved her uncle off after the lift he'd given them to the bustling town. She looked at Zoe expectantly. 'It seems I missed a bit of action on Saturday night.'

'Thea gave us all a bit of a fright but she's all right now thank goodness.'

'Just as well or we wouldn't be here now.'

Zoe laughed, knowing her friend wasn't as hard as she sounded. If Martha had been there, she would have insisted on helping with the clearing up just as Adam had wanted to do. But Julie had seemed about to make an objectionable protest and Zoe had sent them on their way.

'We didn't have many people in yesterday,' she said. 'Simon and I could cope easily so Thea could rest. Today she's like her old self.'

'And you were allowed out.' Martha sounded supremely satisfied.

Zoe was happy too, knowing that Thea seemed none the worse for her collapse. It was good to stand here looking out over the brilliant sea with a clear conscience. Simon had made her promise to stay away from the Lemoni as long as she wanted.

Beside her, Martha fidgeted a little. 'I fancy a long cool drink and something luscious to eat. Adam's told me the very place. What do you say?'

'Sounds good.'

'It's one of the tavernas overlooking the bottomless lake. Come on, I'll show you.'

This turned out to be one of the many that surrounded the lake, and they found a table right on the edge beneath a crimson and yellow parasol.

Martha leaned back in her seat and heaved a sigh a satisfaction.

'Is it really bottomless?' Zoe asked.

'That's what they say, but who knows.' Martha looked mysterious.

Zoe gazed down at the dark water and shivered. 'The place is full of surprises.'

'That's the way I like it. A pretty but busy town built on three hills, a deep lake connected to the sea by a narrow channel with a tiny road bridge over it, a port, lovely beaches and a marina. What more could we want?'

'You sound like a guidebook.'

'That's Adam for you. He grilled me about its attractions when he knew we were coming here. Such a bore. Julie and I came on our first day so I know something about it even if we didn't get much further than the shops.'

'It's useful information.' Zoe thought of Adam's enthusiasm for the places he visited and his obvious desire that others should appreciate them as much as he did. She wondered where he would be heading next.

Their drinks arrived and with them the two luscious ice-cream concoctions that Martha had ordered. They picked up their spoons and set to. When at last she had finished hers, Martha produced a tissue and mopped her brow.

'Poor old Julie, slaving away in this heat. She was late back again last night.'

'Has she found anywhere to live yet?'

'Not that we know of. She clams up when we ask her.'

Zoe frowned. 'Thea thinks her brother will take her in.'

'The charming Dimitri? But didn't you say he lived in some remote place miles away? How likely is that?'

'Not very, I agree. But . . . I don't know.' Zoe thought of the way Dimitri had greeted Julie when they had driven back through town. She had been quick to take advantage of that. In fact it had sounded to her like a strong hint when Julie told Dimitri of her accommodation problem.

'Ah well,' Martha said. 'It's no use worrying about Julie. It's her problem, but I'd be glad to hear she'd found somewhere for my poor aunt's sake.'

'So she's still feeling guilty?'

'And how. But come on, Zoe, enough about Julie. What do you fancy doing now? The shops or some sightseeing?'

Zoe smiled, knowing what Martha's choice would be. 'The shops then. But first there's something I want to do.'

Martha was immediately intrigued when Zoe told her about the art gallery along the waterfront and Dimitri's commission to supply some of his lavish paintings. 'I'd just like to see if any are on show,' she said.

'Then what are we waiting for?'

* * *

A couple of hours later, laden with several bags, Martha steered Zoe towards a small taverna she had noticed on her first visit. This one was overlooking the port, and as they ate their selection of mezes they watched some ferryboats laden with tourists coming and going from the quayside. One in particular drew Zoe's attention. This was larger than the rest, and pure white in contrast to the bright colours of the others that seemed to shimmer in the hot sunshine. Before long it was the only vessel left.

Martha, noticing Zoe's interest, laid down her fork. 'That's the one Adam was telling me about,' she said. 'The *Penelope*.'

'How do you know that? The name's written on the hull in Greek,' Zoe said in surprise.

Martha looked at her pityingly. 'Need you ask? My big brother again.'

'Well, yes, of course.'

'The *Penelope* will be going to Spinalonga this afternoon. Fancy a trip, Zoe? On me, of course.'

'But we've visited the island already.'

'It'll be going to Elounda first, which will suit us. It'll pick up a crowd of tourists there and stop at the island on the way back.'

'You're very knowledgeable.'

'Adam again. I tell him I'll be able to do his job for him when he clears off.'

'He's going soon?' Zoe felt an odd sense of disappointment. She felt she knew Martha's brother almost as well as Martha, but who was she to judge? Her track record wasn't brilliant. She hadn't even had the sense to ask Thea the name of the gallery that was interested in Dimitri's work. It would have saved them wasting time trailing through several and then not being successful in their quest.

'You mean you're planning to stay on here like Julie?' she said.

Martha laughed. 'Not me. I'm into my second week, as you know, and that will be that for a while. I'll come back for a holiday soon, though — a special holiday.'

'How special?'

Martha, laughing again, wouldn't say. She had a secretive look about her now which made her seem much younger than she had a few moments ago. She was like a child trying to keep something to herself but not quite succeeding, Zoe thought.

'I hope he's someone really nice,' she said.

'Would I go for someone who wasn't?'

Zoe, pretending to frown in concentration, looked at her with her head held a little to one side. 'Well, no. On consideration I wouldn't imagine you would. Are you going to tell me anything more?'

Martha hesitated. She picked up her fork again and then put it down with a clatter. 'I didn't mean to say anything, but somehow it just slipped out. You've got a sympathetic sort of face, did you know that?'

'I've never been told that before.'

'I think that's why Adam likes you.'

Taken aback, Zoe stared at her. Was there a touch of condemnation in her friend's voice? They seemed to have got into something deeper than usual here, and she wasn't sure what to say. Martha, though, seemed quite unaware of any undercurrents.

'Never mind me,' she said. 'You'll be one of the first to know if there's anything to tell you, Zoe.'

Zoe, touched, said nothing more for a moment. Out at sea the tourist boats had vanished, well on their journeys to wherever they were going.

Martha smiled. 'What do you say, then, Zoe? Shall we go on board the *Penelope*? It'll be a great way for us to get back, like a mini-cruise. All that sea and scenery, who could resist?'

Zoe certainly couldn't. She and Martha had spent ages wandering up and down the steep streets of the shopping area looking for presents for Martha to take home. Both of them had been exhausted by that and the heat by the time they found this taverna.

'Sounds good, if you're sure.'

Martha grinned at her. 'You forget I'm the sister of the bossiest brother in town.'

'Adam suggested it to you?'

'If you want to put it like that. Bill thought it was a good idea too. It'll save him another journey to pick us up, that's why. What d'you say?'

* * *

They sat in the bows on the top deck and Martha pulled off her shirt to reveal a brief orange sun-top beneath. Then she stuffed her shirt into her bag and produced a tube of sun cream. 'Here, Zoe, have some of this.'

When Zoe had taken some, Martha proceeded to coat herself with it in such vast quantities that Zoe giggled. Martha puckered her nose as her as she put the depleted tube back into her bag. 'I don't believe in taking chances.'

'You look as if you're about to swim the Channel.'

'What, me? Far too lazy, especially in this heat.'

The sun was certainly blazingly hot as they set off, but as they gathered speed the welcome breeze strengthened. They leaned back in their seats, prepared to enjoy themselves.

Soon they left the town behind them and were passing a small island before veering to the left to follow the coastline. The rhythm and movement was pleasant; and Zoe, anxious that the sea would be less calm this far out, felt as relaxed as if she were sunbathing on that beautiful little secluded beach where Dimitri had taken her. She leaned back as Martha was doing, loving it all as they moved along.

And there it was ahead of them, she was sure of it. She sat upright, trying to work out if it really was the same one. It was bound to look different from the sea but she was almost sure. Yes, there was the beach next to it and the jetty. And they were definitely heading towards it now and an announcement was being made over the loud speaker, first in Greek and then in English.

'What's wrong?' Martha said, sitting up too.

'Amazing,' Zoe said. 'I can't believe it. I think it's the beach Dimitri showed me the other day.'

Martha leapt up. 'So we're landing here for thirty minutes? Couldn't be better. Wish I'd brought my swimming things.'

Paddling in the crystal-clear water

was nearly as good in this beautiful place, Zoe thought as they landed and removed their footwear. The water was deliciously cool. She glanced up at the narrow path that she and Dimitri had taken when he had been so angry at the influx of people to a place he had wanted to keep secret. At the time she had felt sympathetic, but seeing it now from the opposite point of view gave a different slant of things.

She told something of her previous visit to Martha now, of how she and Dimitri had watched the passengers land and from the boat spread out to two beaches, and Dimitri's furious reaction to it.

'But anyone can come here, can't they?' Martha said.

'All beaches are public property on Crete,' Adam said.

'I didn't know that.'

'You wouldn't always think so, of course, if you were a tourist here. Dimitri can't really complain.'

Zoe was silent thinking about it.

Dimitri had come here as a child and still felt the same as he had then and about this place. She understood that very well. Your thoughts and hopes from childhood were likely to be with you all your life. She'd read that somewhere and believed it to be true.

'Adam's been hearing rumours about that land next to the Lemoni,' Martha said. 'They might be going to build on it. Did you know?'

Zoe stared at her. 'Simon hasn't said anything, but he's been anxious about something lately. I thought that was because the Lemoni isn't doing too well at the moment.'

'It wouldn't be good for the Lemoni, would it, a building site?'

Zoe was silent for a moment. It didn't sound good.

Martha gave an exclamation of surprise and lifted her leg out of the water. 'I've been bitten. Look, there are hundreds of these little fish swimming about, nibbling at me.'

Zoe could feel them too, little nips

that tickled rather than hurt, but she had more important things on her mind. Simon had been more than a little anxious since she had arrived. Surely he must have heard these rumours too? 'Suppose the new owner has plans to open another taverna?' she said.

Martha stopped splashing about. 'Adam may have heard something more definite by now. I'll ask him. You think it's important?'

'For Simon and Thea, definitely. It could affect their business.'

'Yes, I see what you mean.'

It was odd, Zoe thought, that a place as beautiful as this could have such a depressing effect on her suddenly. With Dimitri she had thought that his change of mood was strange. Now she felt the same lowering of spirits as she had then. This time, though, she was more heavily involved. She paddled slowly to shore and stood for a moment on the warm sand, breathing deeply.

Martha, joining her, looked at the sea and the sunlight glinting on the

Penelope, waiting patiently for them at the jetty. Her mouth was turned down and she shrugged in a deprecating way. 'I'm sorry I mentioned it, Zoe. I don't know what came over me. But I honestly thought you knew.'

12

As she reached the entrance to the Lemoni, a noise from her pocket alerted Zoe to the arrival of a text. She stopped and pulled out her phone. A text from Mum! This was a surprise, as her mother usually preferred speaking to her when she knew Zoe's duties would have finished for the night. The UK time being two hours behind the Greek was proving useful. It was good that she was experimenting with texting now. Zoe imagined her examining her keyboard, frown lines appearing on her forehead as she brushed a strand of hair away from her face.

She opened the message. 'Charles phoned,' she read. 'Refused to tell him your plans. Hope you are well, dear. Love, Mum. XXX'

Brief and to the point. Zoe's hand shook as she clicked off.

The late-afternoon sunlight was trickling through the olive leaves and making bright patterns on the tablecloths. Since no one was about, she sank down into the nearest chair to think about this unexpected development. She had a sudden vision of the stranger's face in the Papia the other day. The lurch of her heart when she had thought for a moment that he was Charles had shaken her. In the painful seconds before she realised her mistake, she knew her efforts to forget him had been futile.

And now Charles was trying to contact her. Suppose he had discovered where she was and how he could get hold of her? He was an intelligent man. He had met Simon and Thea when they visited Bristol after their wedding. He might just have a faint memory of where they were going to live and might assume that she was spending time with them and follow her out here.

Even though it was unlikely, the thought was disturbing. She stared as the moving shadows on the table in front of her and then ran her fingers over them as if she could control their shapes and movements. She couldn't, of course, any more than she could control Charles's decisions, whatever they might be.

She must prepare herself, that was all. He wanted to contact her, that was plain. What wasn't so clear was his reason for wishing to do so. For a wild moment she wished that Mum had asked him why he had made call, but then remembered that she had resolved not to involve her parents in anything more than was necessary.

★   ★   ★

Later that evening, Zoe couldn't help imagining Charles seated among one of the English families that had chosen the Lemoni for their evening meal. Once she thought she heard a deep voice that resembled his and gave a startled gasp, almost dropping the dish she was carrying.

'You look pale, Zoe,' Thea said as she

closed the freezer door. 'There is something wrong?'

'No, no,' Zoe said hurriedly. She could have said that Thea looked paler than usual too. It could be the heat getting to her. Maybe it was just as well they didn't have many people in this evening.

Thea's eyes looked huge in her white face as she gazed at Zoe in concern. 'We are working you too hard?'

Zoe smiled. Thea spoke as if the place was heaving and Zoe was attending to demands that left her in a state of frustrating collapse. 'Not a bit of it. I only wish we had more customers. I've a feeling we're not going to get many more this evening, so I need to make the most of the ones we've got.'

There were several young children among them, mostly boys, who at first delighted in the menu, arguing about what they would choose to eat and changing their minds so often that their parents were soon exasperated.

'I know what we can do,' Zoe said to

them. 'How about the chef giving you tiny amounts of a lot of different things to try out, and then you can choose which you like best if you're still hungry?'

'Brilliant,' said one of the young fathers. 'Then maybe we can have a bit of peace.'

There were only three families, and it looked as if they might be the only ones this evening, but to Zoe's surprise Adam was suddenly there looking tanned and relaxed in his blue shirt and light jeans.

'Martha said I should come,' he confided to Zoe. 'I believe she worried you earlier about that land next door. She wants me to tell your cousins exactly what it was I heard from Petros, one of the boatmen. Not that it's much more than you already know, but she was insistent, so here I am.'

'That's kind of her,' Zoe said. 'And of you too, Adam. Are you eating here?'

'That's the general idea.'

'Then may I suggest that table over there near the lemon tree? Simon's busy for the moment, but as soon as he's free I'll get him to come out to you.'

The children were quiet now, enjoying sampling the selection that Simon prepared for them. He had arranged everything beautifully on a large tray-sized plate for each child, even adding a coloured cocktail stick sporting a tiny Greek flag to each one. Luckily he had thought Zoe's suggestion an excellent one.

It wasn't long before he was free to join Adam. They seemed to Thea and Zoe, attending to the customers, that what they had to say to each other was serious and worrying.

'We hadn't known anything definite,' Thea said to Zoe as she wiped one of the work surfaces in the kitchen before ladling ice cream into pink glass dishes and adding a squirt of something rich and thick from a container from the fridge. 'We think there is someone who doesn't like us being here. Someone who wants us to leave.'

'But who would want that?'

Thea gave an expressive shrug. 'We do not know. Dimitri will say nothing. He could have found out for us but he is silent. Perhaps your friend can tell us more.'

'Go and join them,' Zoe urged. 'I can finish serving these. Please, Thea. It means a lot to you.'

It didn't take long to carry the tray of varied ice creams to the waiting children. She was glad to see that the parents were talking happily among themselves and were content to wait for a while before making their own selections.

She loaded some empty plates into the dishwasher and then returned for more. As she passed the table by the lemon tree, Simon beckoned to her.

'Bring another carafe of wine, Zoe, and then come and join us. You can take my place. You've earned it.'

'He wants you to hear what your friend is saying to us,' said Thea.

Adam smiled at her as she put down the tray she brought and sat down beside him. 'I was telling Simon that Petros is certain that something is going to be happening,' he said. 'His solicitor brother has been involved in it, you see, so he should know.'

'We are very anxious,' Thea said.

Zoe nodded, concentrating on pouring wine.

Adam took the glass she handed to him. 'What's worrying your cousins is not knowing the exact plans for the land,' he said. 'It's peaceful here now with the spare land next to you.'

'He'll take our trade,' Thea said tearfully. 'We have so little. Now we shall have none.'

'It might not come to that,' Adam said uncomfortably.

Zoe leaned forward and took Thea's hands in hers. 'Please, Thea, don't look like that,' she said. 'We are imagining the worst, that's all. It's not certain yet.'

'It's good we know now.' With an effort Thea smiled at Adam as Zoe released her hands. 'Thank you for coming to see us.'

Adam smiled too. 'I hope I haven't

made things worse.'

'It's best to have things out in the open so we know where we are,' Zoe said, thinking of Charles. 'We have to make sure the Lemoni is a huge success for the rest of the season. We'll do some publicity. I'll visit the holiday places further along the coast and have leaflets there for people to see. We'll have special offers . . .'

'Hey, hold on,' Simon said. He had been chatting to the customers but now he came to join them. He reached up to pick a lemon and held it to his nose as if its bittersweet scent could help defuse their anxiety.

'Zoe is right,' Thea said.

Simon put his arm round his wife as she stood up. Seeing them brought a lump to Zoe's throat. 'Come, my love,' he said now, 'we have work to do providing a meal for our kind friend.'

'I'm neglecting my duties too,' Zoe said. 'It looks as if those children have finished already.'

'I know you, don't I?' said a clear

voice at Adam's side.

He turned as a little girl joined the small boy who was standing close to him. 'You were on the island, talking,' the boy said in an accusing tone of voice.

'Was that a bad thing?'

The girl giggled.

'Tansy, Robert, come back here at once and don't go bothering,' called one of the fathers.

Adam waved across to him. 'It's a pleasure. I'd like their company. They can help me choose what to eat if this young lady will kindly do her job and bring me a menu.'

Laughing, Zoe did as he asked and handed it to him with a bow. The other children were clustering round now, all taking at once. She left them to it for a few moments and joined Thea and Simon in the kitchen.

Simon gave her a huge hug. 'That was great, Zoe, finding out about the land so we're pre-warned. What would we do without you?'

'It's not me, It's Adam,' she said. 'And for Martha too, because she made him come to tell you what he knew about it. I'll help you all I can, Simon, you know that.'

'Always a fighter, my little sis.'

'And that's what we need to do — think up something really different to attract the holidaymakers. And local people too, of course. I'll try to think of something, Simon, I promise.'

With the help of his friends, Adam had now made his choice and beckoned to Zoe to take his order. 'It seems I have to have a mixture of rather different items — moussaka for one, and what looks to be some sort of ham and cheese pie, and stuffed fig leaves. On the same plate, of course. Could that be managed?'

By the laughter lines deepening round his mouth, she gathered it wasn't exactly what he would have chosen. She nodded, hiding a smile.

The father of the first two children hailed her on her return from the kitchen, and while she was taking their choices of desserts she was aware that Adam had launched into an account of a ferocious battle that had taken place on Spinalonga centuries before. It seemed to take ages in the telling because of the frequent interruptions from some of the boys. Tansy, the youngest girl, sat eyeing Adam with her thumb in her mouth. Even when Adam's food arrived, the children stayed, hardly allowing him to finish his meal with all their questioning.

Back in the kitchen, Simon handed Zoe a large oval dish brimming with tiny sweetmeats. He looked pleased with himself. 'For those children,' he said, 'with my compliments.'

She smiled at him, noticing the positive way he was standing now instead of with the slight slouch that she had noticed recently. 'Great, Simon. Just the thing.'

His young audience thought so too. The cries of delight that greeted her as she presented Simon's offering echoed round the courtyard and allowed Adam to finish his meal in peace. Zoe removed his plate and asked if he wanted dessert. He shook his head.

'Coffee would be good, though.'

'Greek coffee?'

'If you like.'

'Really?'

'If you'll join me, Zoe.'

'Okay.'

She had got used to the small cups of strong black liquid now that seemed a good end to any meal. An acquired taste but a good one. She had time to sit with him and the children to drink it and it felt lovely to be surrounded by such warmth and excitement.

Then, back in the kitchen, she continued loading the dishwasher before collecting more from the other tables. She walked lightly, pleased with the way the evening had gone even though Simon and Thea's fears were out in the open. When it was time for the party to leave, they called their reluctant children to them with promises to return. There was no doubt they appreciated the pleasant time they had spent at the Lemoni.

'You'll be here tomorrow, Adam, won't you?' the boy called Robert cried. 'We'll come too, won't we, Mum, Dad?'

Adam stood up and brushed a fallen leaf from his shirt. 'If Simon and Thea will have me.'

There was no doubt of that, and Thea's eyes were shining.

'You're a born storyteller, Adam,' Zoe marvelled when they had left and the sound of their voices had faded away. 'Martha never told me that.'

'I try to please.'

'You had them enthralled, and how clever of you to leave off at the most exciting part so they want more.'

His mouth twitched. 'I specialise in cliffhangers.'

And in other things too, Zoe thought, *like kindness and concern for others.*

'Tomorrow you'll be our guest, Adam, if you can find the time to come,' Simon promised.

Adam's smile encompassed them all, but Zoe had the feeling that it lingered on her the longest. She felt herself flush and hastily turned away so that Simon and Thea wouldn't see.

*   *   *

Later still, with all the clearing up done and the courtyard looking ethereal in the moonlight, Zoe sat alone in the courtyard. Simon and Thea had long since gone to bed, but she needed to wind down a little, and what better place to do it was here when she could look out to the dark mountains on the other side of the silvery sea? For a moment she had wished that she could wade out into the calm water to swim for a while in the moonlight and look back at the shadowy trees of the Lemoni. She would cast a wish that it should remain the lovely place in peaceful surroundings that she had come to love.

Now, sitting here instead, the peace gradually stole into her. It had been a beautiful evening following an enjoyable day. She would hold onto her memories of it and be grateful.

13

Adam walked home slowly alongside huge inlet that helped make Elounda the pleasant and sheltered place it was. His time as a temporary guide was coming to an end and he was sorry. Since leaving England he had done many things as he moved from place to place. This one was his best yet. It was only now when his time here was drawing to a close that he discovered that sharing his deep interest in a place and its history by word of mouth was even more satisfying to him than writing about it. In fact it was surprisingly stimulating.

The daily boat trip to the island was an added bonus, and so was talking to Petros, because it made him feel he was a part of the place and not merely passing through. He mustn't forget Hattie and Bill either.

Seeing the way they had settled down to their way of life here was good. Bill had been a bit of a traveller in his work as a business consultant with a UK travel agent's firm, and this was their first chance to choose somewhere to live permanently. Or as permanently as was possible in these changing times. His own widowed mother's death of an unsuspected brain tumour two years ago had made his uncle and aunt think deeply about their retirement plans and what they really wanted. And so they had opted for Crete in the hope of a few years in a place they loved.

'After that, who knows?' Uncle Bill had said, beaming at Adam and Martha when he gave them the news. 'Grab the moment, I say, and Hattie agrees with me. Time enough to worry about the future when the time comes.'

He had been quietly pleased for them while Martha had leapt up and hugged first one and then the other, promising to spend all her holiday with them as long as she lived. They had welcomed him so kindly when he turned up in Elounda a few weeks ago that he had felt at home from the moment he stepped over the threshold of their charming apartment that looked out over the town and the harbour.

It was while chatting to one of their Greek neighbours that he had first heard the rumour about the land next to the Lemoni. He had mentioned it to Petros on his next trip and the expression on the boatman's face as he told Adam the little he knew was grim.

Adam frowned as he reached the harbour. The yellow light from the street lamps made golden ripples on the water among the moored boats. There seemed to be a magic about this place this late in the evening, and yet beneath it all he knew there was something raw and un-defined if you looked deep enough.

Petros had hinted at more than he had told Zoe's relations earlier this evening. This had seemed to him so incredible as to be unbelievable. There was as yet no proof of any betrayal and might or might not be true, and so he had decided it was best kept to himself for the time being. It was bad enough that the site next to the Lemoni could become a building site.

Adam paused for a moment and gazed down at the motionless boats with the tiny ripples of light nudging each gaily coloured hull. He would have lingered for longer, but he knew Martha would be anxious to hear about his evening. She had decided to remain with their aunt and uncle this evening because they didn't feel like coming out. She had pleaded tiredness too after the day in Agios Nikolaos, which they had accepted without question.

He wondered at Zoe's vigour as she moved between the tables. She had looked as fresh and relaxed as if she had spent the whole day resting. Some of her energy must have rubbed off on him as he sat beneath the lemon tree and expanded on some of the ferocious fighting in the area of long ago and of how the Minoans had at last been conquered by the Turks. A bloodthirsty lot, those children, but something had fired their imaginations and he had enjoyed bringing it to life for them.

His intention had always been to make a book of his published writings on his return to the UK while he sought commissions that would send him off round the world again. But for an hour or two this evening he had felt that what he was doing here was far more valuable than the travel articles he was emailing to his editor. Could Zoe's approval have had something to do with that? he wondered. All he knew was that her presence made a huge difference to him, and one he didn't want to think too closely about.

*　*　*

To see the same three families returning to the Lemoni the following evening was heart-warming. Two more joined them, and it was clear that Adam was going to be fully occupied in continuing his lurid tales.

'Are you all right with this?' Simon asked him when he came into the courtyard after the parents of the first family settled themselves.

'Of course.'

No one could doubt that Adam was sincere, but Simon still hesitated. 'It's good of you to come again,' he said quietly. 'But providing you with a free meal isn't nearly enough. We feel we must offer you more than that for giving such a boost to our business.'

'Early days yet. Let's see how it goes, shall we? You're not taking into account how much I'm enjoying myself.'

And Simon had to be content with that because Adam waved aside all hint of payment.

Zoe smiled to see the easy way he gathered the children round him after they had all made their selections from the menu. 'Part one now,' he said. 'Then an interval for this wonderful meal Simon is cooking for us.'

Tansy, the little girl with her thumb in her mouth sat as close to him as she could when the food had been eaten and cleared away. Her brother got up every now and again to strut about as an imaginary Minoan defending territory that had been theirs for hundreds of years. Zoe laughed to see him each time she passed by. The adults chattered quietly to each other as they relaxed over carafes of wine and watched the far mountains dissolve gradually into pink and mauve mistiness as the evening wore on.

Thea looked happier than Zoe had seen her for several days, and Simon's voice was deep with relief.

Martha had arrived now, pleased to see that everything was going well. Zoe joined her at her table in the far corner that was secluded enough to hide her presence from her brother. She wasn't eating, but had ordered a half-carafe of the local wine, and she sat now with her glass at her lips looking at Zoe with laughter in her eyes. Her outfit tonight was subdued, and in the dark colours and the length of her skirt she looked older than the bright young thing of yesterday.

'I don't want Adam to blame me for putting him off his stroke,' she said.

Zoe laughed as Martha passed a glass of wine to her. 'I don't think there's much chance of that. He's been at it all evening. I don't think he'd notice if a tornado hit the place.'

'But would he notice if you weren't here?'

'He might wonder why I wasn't doing my job.' Zoe got up. 'See you in a bit. Stay right where you are.'

As her friend had not long arrived, it was entirely likely. Adam still seemed engrossed, but in the kitchen Thea was already serving up some moussaka for the three of them with bowls of Greek salad on the side. They sat at the kitchen work bench to eat it, and then Adam returned to the courtyard for another story session.

'There's not much more for you to

do here now, Zoe,' Thea said. 'We think you have earned a rest to be with your friend.'

'You're sure?'

'Couldn't be more positive.' Simon grinned at her and gave her a hug with one arm. In the other he held a bunch of spare knives he had collected. He slapped down on the work surface. 'Go for a swim, why don't you? Or a nice long walk together.'

'I might just do that.'

'Brilliant,' Martha said when Zoe joined her. 'I fancy a bit of night life. What d'you say?'

'You're on.'

The town was busier than Zoe had seen it and the atmosphere electric. Music poured out from the harbourside tavernas, and the coloured lights along the waterfront reflected on the faces of the passers-by.

'Where are we going?' Zoe said.

Martha turned a mischievous face to her. 'Where d'you think?'

'I've no idea.'

'Fancy a bit of spying?'

She should have thought of that, Zoe reflected as they headed for the small taverna in one of the streets behind the church.

'So, we're going to check up on Julie?'

'Why not?'

'Will she want that?'

Martha didn't answer but there was a determined look about her that left Zoe in no doubt of her intentions, whether Julie wanted it or not.

The Rosebowl was a narrow building between two taller ones and sported a poster on the open door of a scene of riotous dancers in positions Zoe couldn't believe were possible. A few tables jostled each other on the pavement outside, but there wasn't really room, and the people sitting at them looked as if they had stopped merely for a rest and not for an evening's entertainment. Inside was worse. The stifling atmosphere of chips and oil combined with heavy perfume was overpowering, and Zoe's eyes watered as soon as she and Martha stepped inside.

At first there seemed no space for them, but then a table became vacant near the window. They sat down thankfully and at once Julie was at their side. Her short skirt and brief top were black, and her heels so high Zoe wondered that she didn't topple over had there been room for her to fall.

'It seems like chips with everything here,' Martha said.

'And why not?' Julie was on the defensive. 'People like them. You can't argue with that. They like battered fish too, and mushy peas.'

She looked suddenly weary, and Zoe felt a moment's sympathy for her. Then she remembered that being here was Julie's choice.

'What can I get you, then?' Julie said.

Martha looked surprised, as if food and drink in a taverna, even one as rough as this, was the last thing on her mind. 'Have you found somewhere to live, Julie?' she blurted out. 'Aunt Hattie wants to know.'

A scornful expression flittered across Julie's face. 'What's it to her?'

'She's anxious for you, that's all.'

'You can tell her it wasn't easy.'

'But . . . ?'

'A good place. It'll do.'

'Can we see it?'

'No way so don't ask.' Julie bit the end of her pencil and stared down at the pad in her hand.

'A bottle of mineral water for me, please,' Zoe said to ease an awkward moment. 'And the same for Martha, I think.'

Julie backed away, squeezing herself between the tables on her wobbly heels. They heard raised voices from the back regions, then shouts of laughter. The hubbub around them seemed to Zoe to deepen to a roar and then subside a little. All she wanted to do was escape, but that wasn't possible at the moment.

Julie came back with their order, and with it brought a small plate of sweet-meats and placed it in front of Zoe. 'Dimitri gave me these,' she said. She sent such a swift gloating look in Zoe's direction that she expected him to be somewhere near and glanced round involuntarily.

'He did?'

'Taste them.'

'Thanks.' Zoe passed the plate to Martha and then took one herself. It tasted a little bitter and she wasn't sure she liked it.

'What time do you finish, Julie?' Martha shouted above another burst of noise coming from somewhere behind them.

Julie shrugged. 'Late.'

'How late?'

'One o'clock, two. It depends. Why d'you want to know?'

'No reason.'

Julie left them and they drank their water quickly.

'What a life!' Martha exclaimed as they pushed their way out into the fresh air.

Zoe agreed with her. 'At least you know she's found somewhere to stay even if she doesn't want you to see it.'

'That's only because she leaves it in a mess, that's all.' Martha was unconcerned. 'Julie's the untidiest person I know.'

They walked past the church to the harbour. Behind them the lights in the square shone out over the revellers enjoying themselves near the taxi rank.

Martha yawned. 'That's enough night life for me. I think I'd better be on my way. You'll be all right, won't you, Zoe? There are still masses of people about.'

'Simon said to ring him for a lift but I won't need to bother.'

'You'll probably meet Adam on his way home.'

'I'll see how far I can get before I do.'

'It's been another good day,' Martha said, yawning again.

And so it had, Zoe thought as she started to walk back to the Lemoni. But Julie had seemed odd tonight, as if she had something to hide. And she had been adamant in not wanting visitors at the place she had found to live in.

14

Zoe reached the bend in the road past the harbour, then with a feeling of pleasure saw Adam approaching. He was easy to recognise by his loping stride that seemed to cover the ground between them in minutes.

'I thought it was you,' he said as he came close.

'So Simon and Thea allowed you to escape from the Lemoni?'

'Quite a while ago, to tell you the truth. I found a seat back there. It was peaceful looking out over the sea in the moonlight.'

Zoe could imagine that. He had been with people all day and given out of himself most of that time, and so the quiet time on his own would be wonderful.

'We went to see Julie,' she said.

A flicker of unease crossed his face. 'How is she?'

Zoe considered. Julie had appeared brash and over-confident, but the noisy and crowded surroundings could have been responsible for that. Julie had seemed very much at home, but once or twice she had caught a hunted expression in her eyes that might have hinted at her true feelings. Martha had made no comment as they escaped into the fresh night, air so maybe she was imagining things.

'I'm not sure,' she said slowly. 'I couldn't really tell. Early days yet.'

'Did she say where she's living?'

'It's odd. You'd think she'd welcome a visit from Martha but she wouldn't have it. Refused to tell us point blank. If I were Martha I'd feel really hurt.'

'As bad as that?' Adam looked serious. 'I'll make a point of calling in at the Rosebowl tomorrow and see how things are. The place has a bad reputation but I expect you know that. I don't like to think of her unhappy in any way.'

Zoe thought of Julie's animated face

as she gazed at Dimitri when she turned up late and uninvited at the family party at the Lemoni on Saturday. She hadn't looked at all unhappy then.

'I've a strong feeling Julie's got herself deeper in there than is good for her,' Adam said. 'I'll have a word with Martha. She's known her a good long while and much better than any of us.'

'But what can Martha do?'

'Little enough, I daresay, but it worries me.'

Zoe moved away a little, not liking the way this conversation was going.

Seeing it, Adam looked contrite. 'I'm sorry,' he said. 'I'm keeping you here talking and you must feel shattered. You've had a busy evening at the Lemoni.'

'And loved every minute of it,' Zoe said.

She thought of the attractive courtyard and the views across to the mountains. And of Thea and Simon too, making time to chat to their customers and take a friendly interest in them. Everything that made it so different from the Rosebowl.

They parted and Zoe walked slowly on, meeting others along the way who commented on the beautiful effect of the moonlight on the water. But she hardly saw it. She was thinking of Adam and his concern for Julie.

*   *   *

The courtyard was deserted the next morning when Zoe passed through after her early swim. Usually there was some evidence that someone was about, one or two of the tablecloths removed for washing or the tubs of geraniums newly watered.

She showered and dressed quickly and combed her wet hair back from her face, knowing that the strengthening sunshine would soon dry it.

Downstairs nothing had changed. She made herself a coffee, poured orange juice into a glass, and helped herself to a bowl of Greek yogurt. The container of honey was in the fridge, and as she got it out she saw a note pinned to the lid.

'Zoe,' she read in Simon's bold handwriting. 'We've taken the van and gone to visit Anna and Yiannis. All good news. Back soon.'

She stared at it in surprise. A visit to Thea's parents in Agios Nik at this hour of the morning? But there was nothing to worry about, it seemed. She would just have to wait until they got back to discover the reason.

She lingered over her meal and then took some time clearing it and washing up. A few families passed by the Lemoni and waved to her and then later more came hurrying past, obviously anxious to be on time for the boats to Spinalonga.

Zoe straightened one or two of the tablecloths and then fetched the watering can and gave the geraniums a good soaking. Some of the water trickled onto the ground and she watched it slither away among the dust. A basking lizard came to life and shot across to the small rockery in the corner and disappeared.

At last she heard the sound of the van approaching. It rattled its way down the narrow track between the courtyard and the spare land next door. A few moments later Simon appeared, closely followed by Thea. Both looked radiant.

'We had to tell my parents first of all,' Thea said.

Simon pulled a chair out for his wife and helped her gently into it.

'Such a fussy man, my husband,' she said, smiling up at him.

He beamed proudly down at her. 'I don't become a father every day,' he said. 'Zoe, I hereby declare you are very nearly the first person to hear some astounding news. We're going to have a baby.'

Zoe laughed, delighted for them. She got up and gave Thea a kiss and Simon a huge hug. 'Congratulations,' she said. 'Wonderful news.' She sank down into the seat opposite Thea and Simon.

'We had a bit of a worry earlier,' he said. 'We heard you set out for your swim, Zoe, and then I phoned the doctor. We went to his surgery immediately and he was already there, early as it was. And I'm glad to say all is well. More or less. You were still swimming when we returned, so we headed off to see Thea's mum and dad. You saw the note?'

'I was madly curious.'

Thea's smile lit up her pale face. 'Meetera and Pateras are pleased, very pleased.'

'That's putting it mildly,' Simon said in heartfelt tones.

Zoe got to her feet. 'You'll need to eat, Thea. You too, Simon. You'll need all your strength to cope with it all.'

She had meant it as a joke, but to her dismay Simon looked as if she'd dealt him a huge blow. 'That's just it,' he said. 'The doctor was full of the direst warnings for the next few weeks. It's vital Thea must rest, no question about that, and I've promised to see that she does. And with the season coming on . . . ' He didn't need to spell it out.

'I shall make a solemn promise too,' she said at once. 'I'm here, aren't I? And now my holiday is truly at an end. I'll help you, Simon, to the best of my ability.'

She caught hold of first his hand and then Thea's and raised them to her lips. 'There, that shows I mean it. I promise that for the next six weeks I'm second in command here, working so hard you won't see me for dust.'

She let go of their hands and stood with her hands on her hips looking as stern as she could manage.

Simon laughed and the tension was broken. Thea, too, looked pink with pleasure. 'You are like a sister to me,' she said simply.

'And my first job is to bring your breakfast to you here,' Zoe said. 'Your orders, please, if you will. Or would you prefer to see the menu first?'

They sat there for some time, Simon making an exaggerated show of appreciation of everything Zoe put before them. When they had finished eating, Zoe made fresh coffee and joined them. Afterwards there would be plenty to do concentrating on her new duties, but for the moment she could relax with Simon and Thea here beneath the olive trees.

★   ★   ★

A young couple arrived soon after half past eleven wanting drinks and a rest after their walk from Plaka. As she served them, Zoe marvelled at their stamina setting out on the walk in this heat. An English family of parents, grandparents and three children came for an early lunch soon afterwards. Zoe was pleased that they wanted simple food, merely needing something to fill a gap. She prepared the Greek salads for the adults while the baked beans were heating for the children. Earlier Simon had collected some loaves of bread from the bakery in town. It looked so delicious that it seemed a shame to toast some of it, but so be it, Zoe thought as she set to work.

Afterwards the children were happy on the beach and splashing in the water while their elders watched benignly from their seats in the shade of the courtyard. When she had cleared away and washed up, Zoe gazed up at Simon and Thea's room to check that the shutters were closed. She had insisted that Simon should leave the lunch duties to her as a test of her abilities, promising to call him if she needed help.

'We might get an influx of customers expecting cordon bleu meals,' she said.

Simon had let out a booming laugh. 'Chance would be a fine thing.'

She put her finger to her lips. 'Careful. You'll wake Zoe.'

He had grinned at her and then gone off happily enough. It was good to see him so light-hearted and full of confidence again. Long may it last.

★ ★ ★

Dimitri arrived during the afternoon. His mouth was turned down a little at the corners and his eyes were shifty. Seeing him this early was surprise enough, but his subdued slouch into the quiet courtyard was so unlike him that Zoe felt anxious.

'There's nothing wrong, is there?' she said, coming forward to greet him. 'Julie . . . ?'

'Julie?' he said swiftly. 'Julie has nothing to do with it.'

She wanted to ask him with what, but his manner was too forbidding.

'My sister, where is she?'

'She's resting, Dimitri. Can I do anything?'

He seemed to look right through her. 'My parents, they said to come to the Lemoni. Thea has something important to tell me.'

Zoe smiled in sudden understanding. 'Thea's fine,' she said. 'She couldn't be better. Sit down, Dimitri, and let me get you something to drink. Thea will be down presently.'

A hunted expression clouded his eyes for a moment but he did as she suggested. She could tell he was trying to avoid looking at the spare land next door because his eyes kept flickering towards it and then away again. She looked at it too but could see nothing different about it. The gnarled olive trees were motionless in the warm air and the ground beneath was as dry and dusty as it had always been.

She brought Dimitri a glass of the wine he liked and sat with him at one of the tables. He raised his glass to his lips, looking over at her with an expression that was hard to read. She was toying with the idea of rousing Thea from her rest but just at that moment she appeared, her face suffused with joy when she saw her brother. Dimitri sprang up and she was immediately in his arms, rapid Greek passing between them.

'Such good news,' she added in English. 'We are so happy.'

Zoe left them and joined Simon in

the kitchen. It was Thea's moment and Dimitri's too now, it seemed. Gone was the worried and dejected person and in his place an animated handsome man rejoicing in family news. The change was incredible.

Simon assembled some ingredients on the worktop and set about chopping a piece of meat as if it were his worst enemy. 'There'll be a party to celebrate,' he said. 'The family coming from far and wide. Music, dancing, food and wine flowing and Thea in the middle of it all, exhausted. It's not good.'

Zoe could see that. She frowned. 'But won't they understand she needs to rest?'

'Some will. Not others.'

'And if Thea's not down here in the courtyard?'

Simon shrugged. 'Anybody's guess. They'll rampage up to our room to see why not, I expect.'

Zoe laughed. 'And what does Thea think about a celebratory party?'

'Loves the idea. Says she'll sit over

there under the lemon tree out of the way and keep Dimitri company and let me do all the work.'

'And me too,' said Zoe. 'Don't forget I'm here.'

Simon seemed suddenly to relax. He gave her a broad grin. 'How could I forget that, my generous little sister? And I'm going to be a father!' He picked up the knife again and began to chop in a calmer manner now, Zoe was pleased to see.

'So what can I do now?'

He nodded at a basket of tomatoes. 'Check those over, will you, and then give them a wash.'

Zoe picked up the basket and couldn't resist a sniff of their heady warm scent. She wondered what dish Simon planned to use them, for but couldn't ask because the kitchen phone rang and he leapt to answer it.

15

Thea slept for the rest of the afternoon and part of the evening too. In the days that followed, Zoe marvelled at her patience. She knew only too well how much Thea liked to be at the centre of things at the Lemoni, making sure that everything was just as it should be so that their customers felt welcome at all times. Lying about in the shade was definitely not her scene.

'Her parents are going to look after her in their apartment in Ag Nik,' Simon told Zoe on Friday morning when she returned from her morning swim. 'Anna thinks it by far the best solution and Yiannis agrees.'

Zoe gave him a sharp look. She had the feeling he would rather his wife remained where she was in his safekeeping. 'And what does Thea think about that?' she said as she rubbed at her wet hair with her towel.

'I shall visit her every day after breakfast when it's quiet here. I've been doing her packing and we're nearly ready. You don't mind being here on your own while I take her?'

'I'll ransack the place,' she promised. 'You won't recognise it when you get back. Give me a minute to get changed and then I'll get a breakfast tray ready for her and bring it up. Orange juice and yoghurt with honey?'

His smile didn't quite reach his eyes. 'I don't know what we'd do without you, Zoe.'

She ate her own breakfast in her usual place beneath the lemon tree and had drunk her second cup of coffee by the time Thea and Simon emerged. Thea looked a little flushed and Simon, behind her, looked as if he didn't know what had hit him. She wanted to point out that Agios Nikolaos was only eight miles away and Thea was going to be well looked after, but knew she would be wasting her breath.

Thea flew into Zoe's arms. 'You are a

sister to me,' she whispered.

'And you to me too,' Zoe said, deeply touched.

When they had gone, she set about clearing away her own meal, tidying the courtyard, and giving the pots of geraniums their daily drink.

★   ★   ★

'So you're in charge, Zoe,' Martha said as she flopped down at one of the tables.

'May I get you a coffee?'

'As if you didn't know I'd want one. So where's the boss?'

Zoe made her wait until she had served her and brought a mug of coffee for herself as well before she told her where Thea and Simon were.

'How's it going being second in command?'

'Hard work, but I'm glad to do it. We've had more people in this week thanks to Adam. They know he won't be here tonight though, so it might ease off a bit.'

'My last night.' Martha looked sad for a moment. 'It's a shame you can't come to the small farewell party Aunt Hattie's doing for me. I'm glad to get away for a bit with all the fuss going on. Bill's deep in his olive research, with books spread all over the place when she wants to get on, and the atmosphere's not great.'

Zoe smiled, imagining the scene. Each time the family had come for a meal to the Lemoni, Bill could never resist talking a little about the olive tree and how much it was beginning to mean to him.

'It's Adam's last day on Spinalonga today, did you know? The chap he was filling in for will be back on the job. But not to worry. They've got something else lined up for him.'

'The same sort of job?'

'He's being cagey about it.' Martha took a long drink and put her cup down.

'Another?'

'Why not? It's good coffee.'

When Zoe asked how Julie was getting on Martha shuddered.

'Not good, I gather. Bill's a bit concerned.

He went along to see her but couldn't anything sensible out of her about where's she staying. He thinks Adam shouldn't get too involved with Julie's problems, you see.' She laughed. 'Not that that would stop him if he was really interested, but believe me he definitely isn't.'

Zoe felt a jolt of relief and then was ashamed of herself. Martha didn't stay long after that, just long enough to suggest a visit from Zoe tomorrow afternoon if she could get away.

'You know where Hattie and Bill's place is, don't you, Zoe? They'll be there too, as their friends are off somewhere for the day on their own. My flight isn't till six so there's just time.'

* * *

Zoe found the place easily and was greeted by Martha with a plate of goodies left over from last night's party. She took a piece of homemade shortbread and joined her friend on the balcony overlooking the harbour to the sea and mountains beyond.

'I can see why your aunt and uncle like living here,' she said when she had taken a few sips of the ice-cold orange juice Martha handed to her.

Hattie and Bill had welcomed her to their home so kindly a short while ago, but then had left the girls to their own devices, saying they had a little shopping to do.

'I can't think what,' said Martha, laughing. 'We did a big shop yesterday at the market. Unless Uncle Bill is planning to buy an olive tree, of course.'

Zoe laughed too, pleased by the cheerful atmosphere when it could have been gloomy because of Martha's imminent departure. Her friend's eyes were sparkling and her cheeks flushed, obviously at the thought of a good welcome waiting for her at home. She hadn't spoken much about this special someone, perhaps in deference to her own position with Charles; but now Zoe mentioned him, wanting to know more.

'I shall bring him back with me as soon as I can,' Martha promised when she had filled in a few details.

'For that special holiday you told me about?'

'Maybe.'

'I hope I'm still here.'

'Me too,' said Adam.

Martha spun round. 'Where have you sprung from?'

He held out a pile of books towards her. 'The bookshop, would you believe?' He smiled at Zoe. 'More homework for me, but it's about Gournia this time. One of the hotels is employing me this coming week as a tour guide to some of the local places of interest, and Gournia's the best preserved Minoan town on Crete. We're starting with that on Monday.'

'Rather you than me,' Martha said with a pout.

'Just as well you're going home then, or I'd have offered you one of the spare seats on the coach.'

'Who wants to see a load of old stones on a hillside? Not me.'

'But magical old stones.' Adam's voice was deep with respect. 'On a hillside overlooking the bay of Mirabello.'

'And it's surely more than stones if it's the best preserved Minoan town on Crete,' Zoe pointed out.

Adam smiled at her. 'Would you like to see it, Zoe?'

'On Monday?'

'Tomorrow. I need to recce the place first. Bill's lending me his car for the afternoon and I'd like your company.'

She hesitated and then smiled, remembering that Thea's parents had promised to drive her over after lunch when the Lemoni was likely to be quiet and she presumed she wouldn't be needed for a few hours.

'That sounds good,' she said. 'But I must check with Simon first.'

* * *

Zoe hadn't expected the ruins to be quite so interesting, but with Adam as her guide she might have known the place would seem to spring to life in her imagination.

207

They had left the busy main road between Agios Nikolaos and Sitia and driven up a dusty track until it widened into what seemed to be intended as a car park. Adam stopped the car and pulled on the handbrake. 'This seems to be it.'

They got out into the warm thyme-scented air and saw a wooden kiosk a short way up a narrow path. There was no one else about.

'You've got your bottle of water?' Adam said. 'You'll need it in this heat. I've got spares in the car.' He hoisted a small rucksack on his shoulder.

Zoe pushed her sunglasses further up her noise, adjusted her sunhat and then patted her bag. 'I've got mine in here. I never go anywhere without it.'

'Good girl.'

At the kiosk Adam paid the small entrance fee for them both, and before setting off up a path that led uphill they paused to look an information board with the lettering in both Greek and English. But the heat was such that even Adam found concentration difficult.

'Let's go,' he said with a smile. 'I'll have to see if my research will provide the info we need. If not we'll find out what we've been missing on the way out.'

'I'm happy with that,' Zoe said.

As they began to climb up the widening path paved with large stones, he told her that they were obviously on one of the main thoroughfares, and that the stone walls on either side were thought to be the foundations of the basements of the small houses left empty when the town was abandoned over fourteen centuries B.C.

'There would have been other rooms above and a flat roof that was probably used for sleeping on in hot weather.'

As they went higher up, Zoe gazed around at the maze of ruins that stretched over the lonely hillside. 'It all covers a much bigger area than I imagined,' she said, puffing slightly.

With the sunshine pouring down

from the clear sky, she found it hard going, and soon they paused for the rest that she badly needed. She got out a tissue and mopped her forehead, longing for some shade.

'We'll see the sea in a minute,' Adam said from slightly higher. 'Yes, there it is.'

Zoe joined him and looked too, and saw not far away the shining blue water that almost hurt her eyes in the dazzling heat.

'They think the town might have stretched as far down as the coast,' he said. 'We know that fishing was one of their occupations. Weaving was as well, so they kept animals. Obvious, I suppose. They made pottery too, and did carpentry and metal work.'

'Quite like people do today.'

'Very much like. In fact a lot of the older back streets of the towns and villages today can't be so very much different.'

'Quite a thought,' she said, impressed.

He gave her an intent look. 'You feel it too, Zoe — the magic of the place?'

'I'm so pleased you brought me here.'

'Even in this afternoon heat?'

She was reminded of her water bottle and unzipped her bag to pull it out. She took a long cool drink, thinking of the people living in the small simple houses making their living in the ways they knew best.

'So why did everyone leave if it was such a flourishing place?' she asked.

Adam screwed the lid back on his water bottle. 'Ah,' he said triumphantly. 'The million-dollar question, and one that I'm bound to be asked as a tour guide.'

'And you know the answer, of course?'

'There was a cataclysmic event about the year 1450 B.C., and Gournia was mostly destroyed by fire like so many of the Minoan towns and villages.'

'What kind of event?'

He wrinkled his forehead.

'I don't think that's really known. I'll have to do more research.'

'It was a long time ago.'

'People have been living on this site for about four thousand years,' he said.

'Excavation wasn't started on it until the beginning of the twentieth century. What's so good about it is that very little reconstruction has been done. It makes it all so real somehow, don't you think?'

Zoe considered. 'You mean it seems as if what happened could have been fairly recent?'

'Something like that. It's good that you're asking me these questions, Zoe. I'll know what to expect from the groups I'll be leading.'

'So I'm being useful to you?'

The warm expression in his eyes deepened. 'Can you doubt it?'

Before she could answer he turned away, and she could see by the line of his back that he was afraid he had said too much in those few words. His voice was brusque when he next spoke.

'There's the remnants of a palace up on the top there covering a wide area. I need to look at it all in detail and there will be a lot of standing about, not good in this heat. How about finding you some shade where you can rest while I'm doing it?'

'That sounds good,' she said.

'We can go after that. I think we've seen enough for this visit, don't you? There'll be time for more another day when it's cooler.'

An ancient olive tree growing on the edge of a rocky outcrop was the perfect place, and Zoe sank down beneath it with relief. From here she could see another of the information boards, and in a minute she would go and look at it so as not to appear too ignorant when Adam came back.

For the time being she was content to admire the view of mountains and olive trees surrounding the site. She thought of his uncle's interest in the tree and the way his kindly face lit up when Martha teased him about it. It was good of Martha to text her as soon as she had landed at Gatwick yesterday. But then Martha was like that, so kind and thoughtful.

Zoe couldn't see Adam now, but she

knew he was somewhere near, and because of it she felt surrounded by an aura of peace. It seemed as if this was the place where she belonged, but how could that be in this ancient ruined town? The heat must be doing something to her brain. She pulled out her water bottle and took a long drink. The bottle was empty now. She would have to rely on Adam even more, and that thought was wonderful.

When at last he returned, she was nearly asleep. As she stood up, she saw they were no longer alone and that another couple was admiring the view from the other side of the path. A family of four were starting to climb up from the kiosk.

'This is the most important afternoon of my life,' Adam said in such a low tone she hardly heard him.

'Mine too,' she said.

Neither of them said anything more as they walked down the path to the entrance.

214

16

The wake of the small boat stretched far out on the smooth water. For a moment, Zoe stood watching before wading in for her daily swim. At this hour in the day there was no one about, and apart from the lone figure on board that small vessel she had the early morning to herself. She was earlier than usual because she had slept only fitfully and decided at last that she might just as well get up and start moving. So now she had extra time to enjoy the peace and beauty of her surroundings.

She wondered what Adam was doing now and imagined him rising early too, and having a last look at his notes before setting off for his new job as a tour guide. He was accompanying the group to Gournia this morning, he had told her, and leaving early to avoid the hottest part of the day. Lucky people having Adam to show them round, she thought as she turned to float on her back. In spite of the heat yesterday afternoon, he had made her visit to Gournia so fascinating she wanted to go back there and see more of it. Not with him, of course, because he would soon be off on his travels.

She closed her eyes, feeling the warmth of the rising sun on her face and trying to imagine how it would feel when Adam was no longer here. She would hear news of him from Martha, of course, who had promised to keep in touch. He was a good and kind friend, and between serving their customers every evening at the Lemoni she had enjoyed eavesdropping on his vivid tales of past events. He was brilliant at keeping the children amused while their parents enjoyed their leisurely meals and watched the sun disappear from the evening sky.

At last she turned and swam slowly to shore, but instead of having a quick rub-down with the towel she had left spread out on the sand, she sat down on it with her arms round her legs and her head bent on her knees.

It was hard not to wish for Adam to stay here and continue with the work he was doing. He seemed to enjoy it so much, and his enthusiasm was contagious, and that was lovely. But she knew that travelling the world was his dream. People's dreams were an important part of them, like Simon and Thea's dream of making the Lemoni as successful as it deserved to be. It was wrong of her to wish Adam to relinquish his.

She glanced up and blinked in the bright sunlight. Then she got up swiftly and picked up her towel. In the courtyard someone was already busy, and by the rivulets of water decorating the dust she knew that Simon had started on his daily watering rounds. He came out from behind one of the trees carrying his watering can and looked pleased to see her.

'Good swim, Zoe?'

'As always.'

'So what's wrong?'

She smiled. 'What makes you say that?'

'I've been watching you out there floating on the water looking as if you were asleep. Then you swam smartly to shore and I couldn't see you for ages until now. What's going on?'

She shrugged. 'Sunbathing, that's all. Lots to think about.'

Simon said nothing more until they had decided on what they would have for breakfast and were sitting at a table in the shade eating yoghurt, honey and sweet green grapes. She told him more of the visit to Gournia and of how they had stopped on the way back for ices at a tiny taverna Adam had discovered hidden away on a hillside.

'There was a lemon tree there,' she said, leaning back in her seat and smiling to think of it. 'There were masses of sweet-smelling flowers on it but just one huge lemon.'

Adam had sat with his back to it so he wouldn't be tempted to pick it, and they had joked about the wrath of the owner if he had done so. Just one of the happy memories that would be with her forever, Zoe thought.

★ ★ ★

Simon was later than usual returning from his morning visit to Thea because he stopped off in town on the way back to collect some loaves of bread still warm from the oven. He looked pleased with himself, so Thea must be feeling well.

'I picked up our post too,' he said. 'One for you, Zoe.'

She took the thick envelope from him and saw her mother's handwriting. 'I can't think what this could be.' She looked at it intently and then turned it over as if she would discover some clue there.

'Take your time, Zoe,' he said. 'Everything looks good here, so there's nothing for you to do at the moment. I'll make us some coffee.'

She sat down in the shade of the lemon tree and slit open the envelope. Inside was another one addressed to her in Charles's flowing handwriting, and a short note from her mother saying that the enclosed had arrived that morning and she was sending it on to her at once.

Zoe stared at the second envelope, feeling slightly sick. Then she opened it and drew out a single sheet of paper. She read it through twice, and then with it still in her hand looked across the courtyard to where from this position the leaves of the olive trees half-obscured the sea and mountains. This lovely place seemed a world away from her life at home. It was hard to imagine the rush and the bustle of everyday life back there. She tried to remember the times that she and Charles had wandered hand in hand along the riverside, hardly aware of anything around them in the pleasure of each other's company. It seemed as if she was borrowing a stranger's memories.

Sensing, perhaps, that Zoe needed time and space to consider the contents of her correspondence, Simon brought just a single cup of coffee to her table. She smiled her thanks, grateful for his thoughtfulness. Then she read the letter again. It was short and to the point. Charles regretted their decision to have time apart and wanted them to get back together again immediately and looked forward to seeing her.

Immediately? She gave a dry laugh. Surely Charles didn't think she could drop everything and get on the next flight home just like that. She had promised Simon and Thea that she would be here at the Lemoni for the next six weeks, and she wasn't going to break that even if she wanted to. But then Charles didn't know where she was or what she was doing, she reminded herself. She must be fair. It seemed from what he said that he was still at home and hadn't gone anywhere after all to make the most of his freedom.

She took a sip of coffee and then put her cup down again. She must write to him today. He would be wondering why she hadn't contacted him already after receiving this letter, not knowing that she was a long way from home and she had only just received it. So why not phone him, difficult as the call would be? She owed him that, surely. Her hands trembled a little as she drank the rest of her coffee.

Charles had been right to suggest the separation. She had needed this time apart to realise that staying together would be wrong. He, too, must have had doubts at the time or he wouldn't have suggested it. She hoped that he would accept what she would say to him now and come to terms with it. One day, she hoped, he would find someone with whom he would be truly happy. She got up and carried her cup into the kitchen.

'Problems?' said Simon, busy at his chopping board. The scent of sweet basil filled the air.

'Not a bit of it,' she said, her voice vibrant. She could feel only relief now that she was going to do something positive.

Simon turned to face her, his knife in his hand.

'Put that thing down,' she said. 'It looks dangerous.'

'The letter was from your mum?'

'With another inside it, one I wasn't expecting.'

'From Charles?'

'I need to phone him.'

'Help yourself to the house phone,' Simon said. 'I take it you still want your mobile number kept secret? Remember, though, that we're two hours ahead of UK time.'

She had forgotten that. Another hour to wait, then, to be sure of catching Charles when he took his customary coffee break.

Simon continued chopping as if what she wanted to say to Charles was no concern of his and so he wasn't going to ask. She hesitated. 'I'd like you to know, Simon,' she said. 'Charles wants us to get back together again at once and not wait for the end of the two months. But I don't. And I have to tell him. I'll do that in about an hour.'

He swung round, this time without the knife in his hand. His smile lit up his face. 'So you'll be staying on here?'

'Of course,' said, surprised. 'I promised, didn't I? I'd never let you down.'

'But I mustn't be selfish if you really want to go.'

'No.' She let a pause fall. Then she shook her head, smiling. 'I'm relieved to have the chance to finish it once and for all.'

She took a cool shower, running it for longer than usual. At last she stepped out and dried herself. Her elation had gone now and she felt empty, as if all this was happening to someone else. She couldn't believe how slowly time was passing. Even when she had dressed in something a little more glamorous than her usual shorts, she still had at least fifteen minutes to wait until she could pick up the phone. Plenty of time to select the earrings that would look good with her silk top. In the end she chose some turquoise ones of a similar shade and then gazed critically in the mirror to check.

How ridiculous was this? What would Charles care when he couldn't see her? But knowing she was looking her best made her feel better, and she needed that.

She turned away and gazed out of the window in time to see two boats going past on the calm water on their way to the island. But Adam wouldn't be there to greet them. And soon he wouldn't be at Gournia or other important places on Crete either.

She took a deep breath and gripped the window ledge in a determined effort to put this thought to the back of her mind. It was Charles she must think about now, for a little while at least. She went slowly downstairs.

★　★　★

Afterwards she couldn't quite remember how the rest of the morning passed. She only knew that she had gone out into the courtyard after she had replaced the receiver, feeling shaky and disorientated. For some reason Charles had seemed not to understand what she was trying to say to him, and yet she had been clear enough. They had spoken for only a few minutes when they had been interrupted by what had sounded like the ringing of a bell and the clattering of feet.

It was lunchtime before she thought that the obvious thing to do was write to him. She must wait until she had finished her duties in the kitchen, but while she was busy she practised in her mind exactly what she would say. The words came easily once she had spread out her writing paper on the table beneath the lemon tree and picked up her pen.

She read her letter through carefully before addressing and sealing the envelope. It was done, but she still felt anxious. Maybe that would change once the letter was stamped and she had dropped it into the box outside the post office in town.

At last Simon emerged from his room after his rest and she was free to go out and post it.

17

On Wednesday morning Simon left earlier than usual for Agios Nikolaos and took Zoe with him. It was the first chance she had had to visit Thea at her parents' spacious apartment, and she has cut short her morning swim so that she would be ready in good time. A faint mist shrouded the tops of the mountains, but by the time they were driving up the hill out of Elounda it had cleared. The sky was limpid blue and the sea sparkling in the sunshine. Zoe leaned back in her seat, enjoying the warm air on her face from the open window as they left the town behind them.

'Another hot day,' Simon said with satisfaction as he manoeuvred past a van almost blocking the road as they reached the summit.

Anna and Yiannis greeted Zoe kindly,

welcoming her to their home and saying how pleased their daughter was when she heard she would be accompanying Simon today. Anna looked elegant in her cream dress, and her husband was sporting a deep red shirt and white trousers. Zoe was surprised to see how frail they were both looking, though, Yiannis especially. She wondered that they felt able to look after their daughter, who had been ordered complete rest.

'It is hard for Thea being just with two old people,' Yiannis said.

Zoe smiled. She looked round at the lovely room overlooking the sea and the small island a little way off shore. 'She won't think so for a moment, I'm sure. And to be in this lovely place . . . '

'Beautiful, isn't it?' said Simon.

Anna was anxious that Thea should see all over their home. Yiannis followed them from room to room while Zoe exclaimed over the elegance of it all. They had kept the furnishings to a minimum and she could see how well the place suited them. Afterwards, she and

Thea sat on the balcony beneath the shade from a large oleander and drank long glasses of frosted orange juice while Simon talked seriously with Anna and Yiannis somewhere in the dim regions of their home. It sounded to Zoe as if they were having a furious argument, but Thea assured her they were not.

'So what would they have to argue about, dear Zoe?' she said in her soft voice.

Zoe smiled. 'You? Simon's missing you so much.'

'Meetera and Pateras like having me here, you see. I think they miss the Lemoni too. We talk about it all the time. But they are old and I don't want to be a burden to them. They've been so good to me. I feel better now. I should like to go home.'

'Did Simon tell you that more families come in the evenings now?'

Thea's smile widened. 'Because of the storyteller? He is good?'

Zoe felt her cheeks glow. 'He keeps the children interested, and everyone's happy.'

'Especially you, dear Zoe?'

'I like to see the Lemoni doing well.'

Thea's eyes danced. 'I understand.'

It seemed that she did, but Zoe shied away from the subject. Adam would be gone at the end of the week, and thinking of it was painful. Instead she told Thea about the swimming she still did every day and how Simon was always busy with his watering can when she came into the courtyard afterwards.

Thea laughed. 'He is kind, my husband. He looks out for you.'

When it was nearly time to go, she left him with Thea to have some more time alone together while she went inside to speak with Yiannis and Anna. Both were looking pleased with themselves. Thea looked so well that it was hard to think that she still needed their loving care, but it looked as if Simon was finding it hard to convince them of that.

'Dimitri is coming to see us this morning,' Anna told her. 'He has many new paintings. He wishes to see the owner of the gallery.' She sounded quietly confident, and Zoe hoped she wouldn't be disappointed.

'At last our son is working,' Yiannis said, busy with straightening a painting on the wall. He stood back to admire it.

Zoe moved a little closer. 'This must be one of Dimitri's,' she said. 'Am I right? Those colours are outstanding. And look at the way he's painted those olive trees against the sea. It's lovely.'

Anna looked pleased. 'He is clever. We want him to do well.'

Simon drove past the gallery on the way home, but there was no sign of Dimitri or of any of his paintings on display. Instead Zoe caught a glimpse of Julie rushing along on the other side of the road with a grim expression on her face.

'Did you see that?' she said in surprise.

Simon nodded as they turned the corner and took a quiet road out of town.

'Thea's unhappy about that girl being a bad influence on Dimitri,' he said, 'and worry isn't good for her. She's convinced Julie's stopping him from doing anything worthwhile.'

'But not if he's bringing some paintings to the gallery today, surely?'

'I'll believe that when I see it. It's laziness that stops him working, but it's no use telling Thea that.'

He lapsed into silence and they said no more for the rest of the way. How easily the atmosphere had changed, Zoe thought. Simon had been happy and carefree earlier as they set out for Agios Nikolaos, but now he seemed sunk in gloom. She wondered if it was only because he had left Thea behind — or was there some deeper reason he didn't want to talk about?

*　*　*

In the early evening, a crowd of British holidaymakers gathered opposite the Lemoni, greeting each other with noisy enthusiasm. Zoe recognised one family among them as having eaten here the evening before. Was it too much to hope that they might come again now and bring their friends with them? She stood well back from the entrance with her hand on the trunk of the lemon tree and willed them to cross the road. She smiled as they entered the courtyard and went forward to welcome them. The young mother she had recognised smiled at her.

'We came last night,' she said, pushing her bushy fair hair away from her face. 'Didn't we, Joe?'

'Lovely meal,' he agreed. 'But the kids were disappointed. We're staying at the Napoli and they told us there's a chap here who spins a great yarn and keeps them occupied. Will he be here tonight?'

Zoe hoped so, oh she hoped so, and not only for the reason he had given her. 'We're expecting him,' she said, crossing her fingers behind her back so tightly they hurt.

'We're glad to hear that. So where are we all going to sit?'

'I can push two or three tables together for you if you like. Or shall we seat the children at a table on their own?'

'Good idea. Hear that, kids?'

His answer was an excited clamour. A few minute later the six young children were seated near the lemon tree. Their elders chose to sit where they would have the best view. This was good because from outside it disguised the fact that they were the only customers and might encourage others to come in too.

Adam hadn't arrived by the time Zoe had taken their orders, but the evening was young yet, she reminded herself.

She heard the telephone ringing in the kitchen. 'Adam?' she said when she joined Simon.

'Thea,' he said, his voice ringing with happiness. 'When I go to see her tomorrow she'll be all packed up and ready to come back with me. Anna and Yiannis have agreed if she promises to rest here all the time. I think we'll see to that, won't we, Zoe?'

'Oh yes,' she said, pleased for him and for Thea too.

He turned away, still smiling. 'I wish Adam would come,' she said.

She didn't expect an answer because he was busy with one of the more complicated dishes three of the adults had ordered and needed to concentrate. Outside again she looked anxiously towards the entrance and then pulled out her phone as an idea struck her. A quick text to Martha, easily done. She would understand and do something about if it were humanly possible.

Twenty minutes later, Zoe had a reply to say that Martha contacted Adam and he was on his way. She also gave his mobile number in case Zoe needed it. Good for Martha far away in the UK!

And good for Adam being here too. He gave Zoe a quick smile as he accepted the cool drink she provided and settled himself on the seat she had ready for him beneath the lemon tree.

At first he was drooping a little as if his tour today had been longer than usual, but as soon as the children joined him he brightened.

'So who's been for a trip on one of the boats already?' she heard him say. Six hands shot up. 'Just round the bay, I expect?'

He was contradicted by indignant shouts. 'To the island!'

'Spinalonga?'

'We went there today.'

'No, yesterday.'

'Yesterday and today.'

Zoe smiled as she joined Simon in the kitchen to see if he needed help with any clearing up before she checked on the adults. Soon after that, some more people arrived and she was busy seating them and giving her advice on certain of the items on the menu. One of them, a young man, insisted on ordering in Greek in a pronounced Welsh accent, and this gave rise to some merriment from some of the other guests. The court-yard rang with laughter, and Zoe felt happier than she had since setting out to visit Thea.

★   ★   ★

The evening had darkened now, the afterglow from the mountains fading into grey dusk. The warmth lingered in the sheltered courtyard, and the coloured lights that Simon had strung up in the branches of the olive trees shone down on the faces of the reluctant children as their parents called to them. They were preparing to leave now and scraping chairs back from the tables as they got to their feet. As they finally left, the lighted candle on the table where the Welsh visitors were sitting spluttered and went out.

'Is that a hint that we've got to go too?' the young man said, grinning at Zoe.

'Not unless you can't stand it here a moment longer,' she said, smiling. She picked another lighted candle from a nearby table and presented it to him.

'We might as well finish this delightful concoction of a dessert,' he said, picking up his spoon and waving it at his girlfriend.

'Shut up then, Kevin, and get on with it,' she said.

Zoe brought the extra wine they ordered and Simon came to join them. He usually did this when there were no more meals to cook, liking to chat and to hear the latest news from home. Thea had always encouraged this because the customers liked it too. Zoe joined Adam, and they sat for a little while without speaking and listened to the banter of the others.

'Thank you for coming, Adam,' she said at last.

He yawned. 'Sorry. I must get off. We went to the Samaria Gorge today.'

'A long way away.'

He nodded and picked up his glass to finish the last of his orange juice. 'We didn't go for the hike through it, just for sightseeing. I was with an elderly group who wanted to see it for themselves.

They were an interested lot, eager to know everything I could tell them. And then we went for a meal at a taverna the hotel here recommended.'

'Have you done the walk yourself?'

'I hope to one day.'

The lines at the side of his mouth deepened as he stared down at the ground. She saw that his shoulders slumped a little, and the hand he held on his lap looked somehow vulnerable. He had had a heavy day, but he had come to help them when they needed it.

'And where are they off to tomorrow?' she said, pain tearing at her heart.

'Knossos, I think. They plan a shopping trip into Heraklion after that.'

'Knossos, the biggest and best Minoan site on Crete?'

'Certainly the best known, and with plenty of guides to show people round. But to my mind, Gournia is by far the more interesting.'

Zoe smiled, believing this too because Adam had taken her there. The memory of that lovely afternoon would be with her forever. And so should this moment when she was relaxing at the end of the day with Adam. But tonight there was pain in the dreamlike quality of the quiet courtyard, a feeling of imminent loneliness because he would no longer be here.

Adam sprang to his feet as someone came lumbering through the gap, head bent and shoulders shaking. 'Julie?' Adam called in alarm.

'I had to get away,' she gasped out, and burst into a paroxysm of sobs.

The sight was so surprising that for a second Zoe stayed where she was, unable to move. The scene in front of her was a tableau frozen in time. She blinked as Adam moved quickly to Julie's side.

18

The couple were on their feet now, the young man flexing his muscles and his companion clutching his arm, obviously alarmed.

'No, Kevin, don't interfere.'

'But I must.'

'Please . . . '

'There's something's going on here.'

'But not for us.'

He tried to shake her off but she clung to him.

'We'd better go.'

'No!'

'They'll deal with it. The poor girl's hysterical. We're in the way.'

Reluctantly he allowed himself to be dragged off. Julie was sobbing now with Adam's arm round her.

'What happened, Julie? Why are you here?'

'They said . . . I didn't know . . . I . . . '

Simon looked in despair at Zoe, not knowing what to do. The situation was fast becoming alarming.

'They didn't pay their bill,' was all Zoe could think of to say to him. Not helpful in the circumstances, she thought. She clutched up the pile of paper napkins from a nearby table and thrust them at Julie. Then she pulled a chair forward so that Adam could lower her onto it.

Adam's face as he straightened was pale in the coloured lights and Simon looked completely taken aback. They could do nothing, and neither could Zoe until Julie had calmed down. After a while, Zoe motioned both men away and knelt down by Julie's side. Gradually the racking sobs subsided into a hiccup.

'You came to us so we could help you, Julie,' Zoe said. 'But we have to know what's going on.'

'The work was too much. They were coming on to me a bit and . . . ' Julie took a deep gasping breath. 'I couldn't stand it. I walked out. They threatened me and I was scared. I ran so fast. There were people in the square. I had to find somewhere quiet.'

'Somewhere quiet?'

'I wanted Dimitri to fetch me but he wouldn't come.'

'Dimitri?' Simon's vice was full of anger. 'I knew Dimitri would be somehow involved.'

'But he's not,' Julie wailed. 'Not anymore. He doesn't want me anymore.'

'You were staying at Dimitri's place?'

'My things are there but he wouldn't bring them.'

Zoe heard Simon's quick intake of breath, but before he could say anything she spoke hurriedly. 'Have you eaten, Julie?'

'No, no, I can't . . . '

'But you must.'

Simon, obviously relieved at having something to do, went off to see to this at once.

★ ★ ★

They sat at the table vacated by the family party to eat the moussaka that Simon brought. There was plenty for the four of them because he always overestimated their own needs, and he had this prepared in advance for them. The problem facing them, of course, was somewhere for Julie to stay while she decided what to do. Adam put down his knife and fork, most of his food untouched.

'My aunt and uncle might be able to help,' he said. 'But I'm going to be moving on at the end of the week and they're planning a trip away when I leave. They're a bit flustered about it all because of the worry about Hattie's aches and pains.'

Simon pushed his plate away. 'I'd better get on the phone to Dimitri. He'll have to answer for this.'

'No!' Julie sounded frantic.

'But something must be done,' Zoe pointed out as she collected their plates and placed them on a nearby table. 'We've only got two bedrooms here, unless . . . ' An idea struck her. She had often wondered what sleeping in the open air would like. It was warm enough for her to do that here.

Adam got to his feet. 'I'll make a phone call,' he said. He moved across to the lemon tree, and by the time he returned Julie was sprawled half across the table, half asleep. 'She's the only one not showing any concern,' he said as he sat down. 'And I can't help either. Hattie's had a fall and is shaken up. Bill doesn't think they can cope. I'm sorry. I feel responsible.'

'Then I shall sleep down here,' said Zoe, 'and Julie can have my bed for tonight.'

In the end they settled for that, although Simon tried to insist that he should do so instead. But Zoe had been adamant and taken Julie upstairs to her room and bundled up some clean clothes for herself for next day. Julie was asleep almost at once, murmuring that she wanted to stay there forever.

And that was the problem, Zoe

thought as she crossed the road in the dark silence and scrambled down onto the beach. Maybe they wouldn't get much more sense out of her than they had this evening. Adam had left looking deeply unhappy, and what Simon wanted to do to Dimitri she could only guess. And Thea, who needed rest and quiet, was due home tomorrow.

Zoe had made up a bed for herself beneath the lemon tree, piling cushions on the ground for a mattress. But the thoughts were whirling in her head and she wasn't ready to settle down for the night yet. Instead she had come across the road to sit for a little at the edge of the water to watch the moon rise above the dark hills on the other side. It came, a huge orange ball, and the sea welcomed it with a path of golden radiance. A beautiful, humbling sight she hadn't seen before. She marvelled at how quickly it seemed to rise in the sky, smaller now and silver so that the narrow path on the sea below rippled with shiny light.

Zoe slept later than usual the next day and woke with a start to see the sun higher in the sky than she expected. She leapt up and bundled up her bedding. No swim for her this morning, but a quick wash and dress in the bathroom before anyone else needed it.

Simon appeared, looking tired and drawn. He hadn't yet shaved and his T-shirt had a patch of oil on the left sleeve.

'You'd better not let Thea see you looking like that,' Zoe said.

'Any sign of Julie?'

'Not a sound.'

'What are we going to do, Zoe?'

'Carry on as usual? Water the plants, have breakfast . . .'

'At a time like this?'

'It won't help anything if we don't.' Zoe was aware that she sounded like a brisk governess with a wayward child, but she couldn't help herself.

Suddenly he smiled. 'Right as usual,

Zoe. I'll get the watering can.'

By this time Zoe had whisked off some of the stained tablecloths and replaced them with crisp clean ones. The bitter-sweet scent of damp geraniums floated in the air. Then she went upstairs to check on Julie and push open the shutters to let in the light. She was beginning to stir.

'You'll need to get up soon,' said Zoe, smiling her encouragement. 'Breakfast will be ready downstairs.'

'What?'

'Come on, Julie. We haven't got long.'

She left her to it and went down to the kitchen to prepare coffee and get the bowl of homemade yogurt out of the fridge. She took her time over this and then carried a laden tray out into the courtyard.

Simon had shaved now, and his white T-shirt looked new. He chose to sit at the table near the entrance as far away from the kitchen as he could, as if distancing himself from the action he suspected to erupt within the next few minutes.

But it didn't come. Instead, Julie appeared wearing her clothes of the night before. Her face was pale, but she looked calm and self-possessed.

Zoe pulled a chair forward, relieved to see her. 'Come and sit down, Julie. Are you feeling better?'

'I want to go home.'

'Then I shall phone Dimitri at once to bring your things,' Simon said, getting up a little too eagerly. 'If he's not at home now, he should be.'

'Bring another cup,' Zoe called after him.

She saw now that they had visitors, the Welsh couple who were with them last night. Both looked shamefaced as they entered the courtyard. 'We don't usually leave a place without paying the bill,' the girl said rather breathlessly.

Her companion nodded. 'Your fault, Bronwen. It was you who dragged me away.

'We don't blame you for forgetting,' Zoe said, smiling as she got up to accept their money. 'It was good of you to come back so quickly.'

'We couldn't sleep.'

'Our guilty consciences at work, you see.'

'But you're here now,' Zoe said with satisfaction.

'And everything's OK?'

'Couldn't be better,' Simon said, returning to them. 'I think this calls for a reward, a special discount when you come again.'

'Great, we'll hold you to that.'

The feel-good atmosphere they left behind was pleasant while it lasted, even though there was an underlying anxiety still. Once or twice Simon glanced at his watch before questioning Julia about her plans. She could tell him little except that she wanted to get away from a place that had brought her only unhappiness.

When they heard a car drawing up outside, Simon was on his feet at once. A car door slammed and Dimitri came into the courtyard looking thunderous. He threw an overstuffed bag towards Julie. 'It's all there.'

'All of it?'

'Check if you don't believe me.'

'No need to be like that, Dimitri,' Simon said. 'You threw her out.'

'And not before time.'

'What do you mean by that?'

Dimitri's shrug was so expressive there was no need for further revelations. But it angered Julie. 'Look who's talking,' she cried. 'Dimitri, the charming family man, frantic for that place up in the mountains and willing to do anything to get it!'

'What are you talking about?' Simon said.

Julie turned on him, her face flaming. 'You didn't know he had this shady arrangement with his pal to provide the money to buy that land next door in exchange for his share of the mountain cottage he was desperate to have, even though it would harm the family business?'

'Say what you like.' Dimitri's voice was full of malice. 'No one believes you.'

'They will when it happens.' The venom in Julie's voice sent a chill through Zoe.

The moment's deep silence that followed seemed to go on forever. Zoe cleared her throat. Dimitri looked suddenly deflated, and in that instant she saw something in his expression that made her wonder. He sank down into the nearest chair.

'At least you can drive me to the airport,' Julie cried.

'I shall do that,' Adam said.

★　★　★

They left soon after; and Simon, obviously relieved, got ready to go off to Agios Nikolaos, where Thea was waiting for him to bring her home. There was plenty for Zoe to do, too, to make the Lemoni extra welcoming.

Dimitri stayed where he was, and Zoe made coffee for them both and carried it out to him. 'Let me get this straight,' she said, looking down at him.

'You knew that your friend wants to build his own taverna on the land next door, a bigger and better one than the Lemoni?'

'What if he did?'

'Did?'

'Yes, did.'

'Don't you care about Thea and Simon? How can they continue to make a go of this with opposition like that?'

'You know nothing.'

'You're a monster!'

'You think too badly of me. I wanted that place away from them all. I needed it, and it was time for a change. They knew it.'

Zoe waited, her thoughts whirling. Dimitri would do anything to get what he wanted and was prepared to do his family down in the process. 'You disgust me,' she said.

He got up then and threw the contents of his cup at the trunk of the nearest olive tree. The coffee slithered down the trunk and lay on the dusty ground beneath in a dark pool of liquid.

Zoe froze. She had gone too far. But instead of rounding on her, Dimitri said quietly, 'They have nothing to fear. I must leave my mountain cottage. I shall go to Heraklion, far away.'

He turned on his heel and left.

And now the silence was unbearable. She should have been thankful that Thea need know nothing of this; that everything could seem normal when at last she came home. Simon still seemed shattered when he drove off, but by the time he got to Agios Nikolaos this should have worn off in the delight of collecting his wife.

But she could think only of Adam's drive to the airport and the long wait he would have before Julie managed to get a flight to the UK. She had no doubt he would wait with her, however long it took. Except that he had to pack his own things ready to set off himself. And he had Hattie to worry about too, and Bill being able to cope.

Suddenly it was all too much. Zoe sank down at the table with her head on her arms as the tears came. At last she raised her head, surprised to see that the courtyard looked just the same, with the table she sat at needing clearing. The sounds of traffic in the road outside were louder now, though, reminding her that Thea would soon be here.

She dried her eyes on one of the discarded napkins and got unsteadily to her feet.

19

Adam came as he said he would, looking in his blue open-necked shirt the same Adam she had come to know these last few weeks. And yet there was a difference in the way he looked at her, as if he was half-afraid of her reaction now the secret about the Lemoni was out. In someone else she might had thought it was shyness. His eyes never left hers, even though she felt the gnarled branches of the ancient olive trees behind them in the spare land were magnetic.

'You'd do this for me?' Zoe marvelled.

'That and a great deal more.'

She could see that he meant it by the light in his eyes and the serious tone in his voice. His mouth turned up a little at the corners, though, and the next minute they were laughing and she didn't quite know why.

She stopped suddenly and wiped tears from her eyes.

'Adam?'

'Zoe?'

'This is real, isn't it?'

Then his arms were round her and she relaxed into them as his lips found hers. She felt his reluctance as he released her, and for a moment his expression as he gazed at her was unfathomable. 'There's one thing, my dearest Zoe, You know I have to leave?'

She hesitated, looking up into the leaves of the lemon tree that were motionless against the sky on this lovely calm evening. Soon dusk would come, quickly and with little warning, and the lights that Dimitri had helped to install in the branches overhead would light the warm night air.

Adam was leaving. Charles had gone, and things had never been the same between them since. Now she had sense enough to see that her freedom was the most valuable thing that Charles could have given her. He had been honest and brave in making a decision that was right for them both.

She smiled. 'I know you have no choice.'

His gaze seemed to penetrate her very soul. 'And I have a choice about returning?'

'Maybe.'

'But if you're no longer here?'

'You'll know where to find me.' She could say that with confidence, secure in the knowledge that however far Adam chose to roam, he would return to her and be glad to be back. And she would welcome him.

'Let's walk,' he said, taking her hand.

The afterglow hazed the distant mountains in shimmering mauve. She had never seen them more beautiful.

We do hope that you have enjoyed reading this large print book.

Did you know that all of our titles are available for purchase?

We publish a wide range of high quality large print books including:
Romances, Mysteries, Classics
General Fiction
Non Fiction and Westerns

Special interest titles available in large print are:
The Little Oxford Dictionary
Music Book, Song Book
Hymn Book, Service Book

Also available from us courtesy of Oxford University Press:
Young Readers' Dictionary
(large print edition)
Young Readers' Thesaurus
(large print edition)

For further information or a free brochure, please contact us at:
Ulverscroft Large Print Books Ltd.,
The Green, Bradgate Road, Anstey,
Leicester, LE7 7FU, England.
Tel: (00 44) **0116 236 4325**
Fax: (00 44) **0116 234 0205**

NOT INTO TEMPTATION

Anne Hewland

Rejected by local landowner Sir George Foxcroft, Hannah Brockley opens a girls' school in the family home to achieve financial security for herself and her sister Margaret. But then one of the older pupils dies in suspicious circumstances. Both the sympathetic Reverend William Woodward and the handsome Dr Shipley were present that night. Will they help Hannah through a perilous spiral of danger and deceit to find the happiness she seeks — or could one of them be implicated in the crime?

FALLING FOR A STAR

Patricia Keyson

Thea loves her job in TV, but hates her boss Hermione. When Thea gets a chance to interview her favourite movie star, Justin Anderson, Hermione is willing to do anything to sabotage the blossoming romance between her underling and the handsome actor. Then Thea gets the chance to stay in Justin's country mansion and do some in-depth research. But is he really as nice as he seems? And will she become just another one of his easy conquests?

THE POTTERY PROJECT

Wendy Kremer

Commissioned to assess the Midland Pottery Company's financial prospects, Craig Baines faces an angry manager — Sharon Vaughan has had no warning of his arrival. The workforce soon accepts their well-meaning visitor, even though they know his findings could result in dismissals. When Craig detects that someone is pinching china and pitches in with Sharon to help solve the crime, she becomes increasingly aware of her attraction to him. But after his report is complete and he's about to leave, has she left it too late to let him know?

A SURPRISE ENGAGEMENT

Pat Posner

Flora can't understand how she let her best friend, Val, persuade her to pretend to be engaged to Val's brother, Bryce Torman, heir to the Torman estate. It's only supposed to convince their Uncle Hector that Bryce is serious about someone other than the singing star, Jilly Joy, he's recently been spotted with. To make matters worse, Flora and Bryce have got on like chalk and cheese since childhood — and yet Flora finds herself enjoying his 'fake' kisses rather more than she ought to . . .

MARRIED TO MEDICINE

Phyllis Mallett

Dr Linda Shelton lives a quiet life with her mother, who boards medical staff from the nearby hospital. Linda's life revolves around her career — until Dr Martin Crossley arrives at the hospital and takes a room at Shelton House. It's clear he is attracted to Linda, and eventually she reciprocates — but their budding romance is soon tested. Mrs Shelton faces a seemingly unsolvable problem — and, when it all comes right, nothing will ever be the same again . . .

THE CARING HEART

Sheila Spencer-Smith

Caro has always looked after her niece Rose, who is like a sister to her. With Rose threatened by an unpayable rent increase, Caro heads off to the Hovercombe Manor estate to support her and sort things out. On her way, she meets Liam Tait, the attractive new owner of the Manor, and starts to fall for him. But the scheming of the unpleasant estate manager Jared, and the arrival of Liam's gorgeous friend Elissa, both spell trouble for Caro . . .